The Librarian's Monsters

BOOKS & MONSTERS

EVE NEWTON

The Librarian's Monsters
Books & Monsters

By Eve Newton

Copyright © Eve Newton, 2022

One

Kate

BITING MY LIP, I sink further into the comfortable chair behind the counter in the Eastville Public Library. I wiggle a bit, my cheeks heating up at the risqué nature of this novel, hidden inside a magazine. It's late-night opening, so it's already dark out and with only one patron left, I plan on leaving here as soon as she is finished.

Doris is an elderly lady with a penchant for steamy romance, so when she plonks down three books that would burn a hole in your bookbag they are so hot, I'm not surprised.

"You read any of these?" she asks, stabbing them ferociously.

I shake my head and stash my book-slash-magazine under the counter and stand up. "I haven't," I say.

"Oh, you should," she says, "Nothing like a good bit of steam to get the blood pumping," she adds with a lewd leer.

I clutch my fake pearl necklace and force a smile on my face. "I'm sure," I murmur and then check out the books, piling them up and pushing them closer to her. "Goodnight, Doris."

"'Night Kate," she says, scooping them up and dropping them in her bookbag. "See you in a couple of days."

I nod and wave to her before sinking back to my chair and snatching up my book. It's a smoking hot paranormal romance with monsters and a heroine who takes them any way it's given. I would never admit it to anyone, but I find them as arousing as Doris finds her favored smutty contemporary billionaire romances. I'm head Librarian here in this small town, and I take that role very seriously. My guilty pleasures are for me only to enjoy. They bring a spark of heat to my very unoriginal life. My parents died in a car crash five years ago. I was only twenty-five then, and it felt like the end of the world. I was devastated and it took me a very long time to come out of my room after it happened. No one understood. They all said time heals all wounds and that I would get over it.

I haven't.

They were my best friends and my biggest supporters. I still feel empty without them. I isolated myself and after a year, I lost all my so-called friends and there is no family left to speak of. But that's fine. I like my own company and I have my books. I have *all* the books. This library is the biggest for miles around and I'm proud to work here, to be head Librarian here.

"I will see you again tomorrow," I murmur to the book and stash it in the cupboard under the till that I can lock away. I never take them home. These are my special treat for when I have a few minutes at work, especially on late-night opening when it is usually very quiet.

I turn the key and pull it out. Straightening up, I gather up my bag and jingling the keys, I head to the front door.

Locking up after I've set the alarm, I turn right and walk down the street to my home a few minutes away. It is a small house, but it's cozy and it's mine and I won't ever move unless I'm forced to.

Once inside, I take a slow breath in and then exhale quickly. I'm not hungry, so I kick off my shoes and head upstairs to my bedroom. Walking up to the dresser, I reach out and slowly pull the small sheet from the mirror. I avoid looking at myself while I take my glasses off and remove the pearl necklace that was my mother's. Then I force myself to stare at my reflection. I gulp. I look just like she did. Everyone said so. Even I can see it.

And I can't bear to look at myself. I'm only doing it now to see if I look any different. Tomorrow, I turn thirty and it is also the day my parents died. I won't be celebrating it. It's just another day. But I wanted to see if I looked any older, any different to the last time I checked.

I don't.

I strip off my white blouse and black pants, staring at my body. I'm not fat, but I'm not skinny either. My breasts are fairly small, my stomach is a bit jiggly, and my thighs meet in the middle, but I don't care. I will never be a size zero and if I gain too much weight, I'll just buy more clothes. It really doesn't matter to me.

I am exactly the same as I was a year ago in both appearance and my routine.

A creature of habit by nature, I don't like it when things change. It is a source of stress that I don't want in my life. Every day, everything is exactly the same.

I replace the sheet and turn from the dresser to get undressed. I snuggle into my comfy cotton pjs and then climb into bed with a yawn. Grabbing Jane Eyre from the nightstand and slipping on my old glasses, I pull my long dark hair out of the ponytail and settle down to read for the night.

I wake sometime later with the lamp still on and my book on my lap. My glasses are still resting on my face. Glancing at the clock, I see it is 1AM.

A sudden sob escapes me, creeping up on me when I least expect it. Only today, I should expect it. I take my glasses off and curl up in a ball, pulling the covers over my head and letting the grief wash over me. I let the tears roll down my cheeks and hope that I fall back asleep as I have done numerous times in the past, glad that I am working later on to distract me as much as possible from this awful day.

Two

Kate

MY ALARM BEEPS at 7AM which is usual for a Saturday morning when I need to get up for work. I work six days a week. I would work seven, but the library is closed on Sundays. Opening my eyes, I groan. They feel gritty and sore and I'm tired and aching, but I climb out of bed and head for the bathroom.

Twenty minutes later, I'm ready for work and yawning, I make my way to the kitchen for breakfast. I'm famished after missing dinner last night. Opening the fridge, I pull out a big piece of chocolate cake. This will be my only acknowledgement of what today is. Sitting down with my tea, I stuff the cake into my mouth with a delight that borders on happiness, until I remember what this day also is and my elation crashes back down. I push it to the side and place the dirty plate and cup in the dishwasher. I check my phone for the time and decide I can be early today. It means I can get a bit of quiet reading in before Sandy comes in for her shift.

5

Rushing so that I get in quicker, a few minutes later I'm opening up and then frown when the landline rings. There is only one reason the phone would ring this early. Groaning, I pick it up and as expected, it's Sandy coughing on the other side.

"Kate, I'm sick. I can't make it in today."

Cough-cough.

I roll my eyes and purse my lips. I should've known this would happen. It just so happens to coincide with the ladies night last night at the new bar down the street.

"Okay, fine," I say in a world-weary voice. There is no point arguing about it.

"Uhm. Okay," she stammers, not having expected to get away with it so easy. "See you Monday."

"Sure," I comment.

Replacing the phone, I look around. I have all day in here by myself, and it's usually quiet on a Saturday. Grinning, I duck around the counter and pull the key from my bag to open up the cupboard under the till.

Before I can retrieve my book, the phone rings again, this time an old lady asking what time we close today.

"Midday, as always, on a Saturday," I remind Mrs. Peterson.

"Right," she says.

With a grimace at a strange beeping coming from the till, I hang up and go to investigate.

And that is the start of the Saturday that never ends.

I'm rushed off my feet until gone 1PM, an hour past the time we are supposed to close. I haven't even replaced all the books that came back in this morning, but decide that I'll come in tomorrow and get it done. I'm tired from lack of sleep last night and being so busy this morning. I want to go home, take a nice hot bath and to help with my mood, I'm taking my sexy Monster book home with me as an extra special treat. I've been left hanging at the start of a Monster orgy which is going to prove to be my undoing, I'm sure.

Bending down to finally retrieve my book from the cupboard, I see something odd.

"What's this?" I murmur, picking up an old iron key. It's huge and heavy. I balance it on my palm. "You weren't in there yesterday, I'm sure of it."

I close my fist around it and snatch up my book, still covered by the crochet magazine. Closing the cupboard, I examine the key, but have no idea where it came from or what it fits. It must've been in there yesterday. I was the only one here.

Shoving it and the book in my oversized bag, I snatch up my phone from the counter and leave the library, locking up behind me, determined to be back first thing to tidy up all ready for re-opening on Monday.

I cast a glance up as I walk down the street towards home. It has gone very windy, which is strange in Spring. I brush my hair out of my face and carry on walking, putting my head down and gripping the handle of my bag. All of a sudden, I feel a rush of air right behind me. I turn towards it and see the visible ripple coming towards me, and wash over me, taking my breath away and making me gasp.

"Kate!"

I hear my name being called, so I turn around again, but I don't see anyone. In fact, the streets are deserted, which is highly unusual on a Saturday afternoon in the middle of the town.

"What the...?" I mutter under my breath. Something weird is going on, but I have no idea what. I'm out of the loop if there was a severe weather warning mentioned.

I pull my lightweight jacket closer around me and head

down again, I thrust myself into the gale that is blowing all around me. I need to get home quickly.

"Kate. Kate. Kate."

I hear the chant of my name over the noise of the gusts and shiver. There is *no one* here.

"You're losing it, Kate," I tell myself, and pick up my pace, practically running the rest of the short way home. I fumble with my house keys, dropping them in my haste to get the door open, convinced now that someone is following me. Bursting through the front door as soon as I manage to get it open, I slam the door shut and lean against it, out of breath and windswept. I must look even worse than I did this morning with my hair all over and my cheeks flushed from the wind. Not that I'm going to look, nor do I care, but it's just a remote observation. Pushing off from the door as my breath steadies, I slide the bolt into place and feel much better than I did outside.

I pick up the remote as I walk into the sitting room and flick on the TV to see if there is any news about this weird weather system that has moved in.

No signal.

Checking my phone, I discover that it is also out, but it doesn't surprise me with the force of the gales outside.

"Well, book. Just you, me, a glass of chilled white wine and a hot bath. How does that sound?"

Grabbing the book from my bag, I head upstairs via the kitchen for my afternoon glass of wine and then to the bathroom to run an extra hot bath. The temperature has dropped significantly with the weather storming outside, and I shiver when I get undressed. Placing the glass on the corner of the bath, I climb in and carefully pick up my book, holding it up so as not to get it wet, and settle down to the welcome distraction of a dirty Monster orgy that leaves me as breathless as the wind did outside and hotter than I can credit the cooling bath water with.

Three

Kate

THE NEXT MORNING, I wake up extra early and get ready to go to the library. It will be lovely and quiet, and I can replace my book on the shelf without anyone knowing I'd taken it out and read it.

I blush when I think of the scenes I read last night. Definitely got me all hot and bothered. It has made me realize that I could do with more excitement in my life.

Sighing, I open my front door and then remember the weird weather from yesterday. All is calm now but very quiet. There are no dog walkers out or Sunday morning joggers. It must've spooked everyone, not just me. But seeing as I have a signal on my phone now, it isn't bothering me so much.

I walk quickly to the library and slip inside, relishing the dark and quiet. Taking the Monster book out of my bag, which I dump on the counter, I place the book on the trolley full of yesterday's returns and wheel it over to the stacks. I lovingly replace book after book, making sure that shelves are neat and tidy, and the titles are in alphabetical order by author.

When it comes to replacing my sexy book, I reluctantly slide it back into place and then freeze.

"Kate."

I look over my shoulder, but there's no one there.

I'm losing my mind.

"Kate. Kate. Kate. Pretty, pretty Kate."

"Okay, who the fuck is there?" I snap, suddenly getting pissed off, my face heating up from the irritation.

Silence.

"Sure, make me look like a lunatic talking to myself," I murmur and then turn to the right to wheel the trolley to the next aisle.

"Aaaaah!" I shriek at the creature looming over me at the end of the aisle. He is really tall and exactly like one of the Monsters from my book. Horns, tail, sharp teeth, claws... "Aaaaah!" I scream again and turn to run in the opposite direction, only to slam straight into another creature who looks identical to the first. "Fuck!" I yell and spin, but I'm blocked in by the twin Monsters on either side of me.

I scream my head off when the tail of the one I'd run into, lashes out and catches me around the waist, lifting me off my feet. I struggle and scream, completely helpless in the grip of the Monster.

"Kate," a quiet, calm voice says my name. It's soothing and beautiful and has the desired effect. I stop struggling and look over to where the voice is coming from.

I blink when an eye-wateringly gorgeous male approaches me. He has dark hair and blue eyes and a calming presence that I'm desperately in need of right now. Thinking that, reminds me of the Monster who has his tail wrapped around me and I start screaming blue murder again.

"Kate," he says again in that scrumptious voice. "You have no need to be afraid."

"Yeah? Easy for you to say," I yell, struggling again but it's completely pointless. I'm not even that afraid anymore, just pissed off.

That is until, Mr. Smooth reaches out with his hand and his normal fingers turn into long sea-green tentacles that wave around in front of my face, before one of them strokes me, the little suckers on the underside, suckling my skin and with a cry of disgust, everything goes black.

Sometime later, I open my eyes and blink once, twice and then groan. I try to bring my hand to my head, but I can't. I'm restrained.

"I apologize for scaring you," Tentacle guy says. "That was not my intention. Usually, I can soothe anyone..." He gives me a perplexed expression which does not help the hysteria which is rising up.

I giggle.

It then turns into a full-blown laugh that hurts my stomach and my already aching head.

After a few seconds, Tentacle guy clears his throat.

"Indeed," he murmurs. "My name is Thrace. You have no need to be afraid of us, Kate. We aren't going to hurt you."

"Much," one of the twin Monsters mutters.

Thrace turns to give him a filthy look. "Quiet," he snaps and then with a smile back at me, he says, "Ignore him. He is a beast."

"No shit," I mumble, the swear words coming thick and fast. "Is this a dream? A nightmare?" I recognize them now that I've had time to think, but Thrace was not the name of the tentacle guy in the book.

"No, we are very real, oddly. This is as surprising to us as it is to you."

"Where did you come from?" I ask cautiously, wiggling my arms to try and get out of the restraints. All it does is stretch my red blouse tighter over my breasts, which is noticeable to Thrace over on the other side of the room.

I swallow and plan my exit out of the back office where they tied me to my office chair. The twins are kind of blocking my way though, stationed on either side of the door. Panicking though will get me nowhere and Thrace seems to be reasonable, at least in the sense where I can talk to him. The twins seem way more feral – naturally.

"The book," Thrace says, bringing his eye back up to mine.

"How? And why do you have a different name?"

He waves his hand dismissively. "That is just the name of our characters. Our real names are different. Our real *lives* are different. And that's what we need to find out. We would like to go back."

Hmm, interesting.

"Yeah, I bet you would," I snort, now thinking of the orgy I read about last night.

He gives me a curious look.

I feel the annoying need to explain myself. "Your heroine is probably missing you," I stammer, suddenly shy again.

He chuckles. "You are the heroine, Kate," he says.

"Err," I murmur, "what do you mean?"

"The reader becomes the heroine. There is no real heroine to the story, only those who read about us in the books."

"What?" I spit out. "That makes no sense. For that to be the case, you would have to be *real* in the books..." That can't be right. Can it? I know books are magickal, but *this* magickal? "So you are saying you have a life *inside* the books?"

He nods warily, probably wondering how much to tell me.

"So how do you go back?" I ask, accepting completely what he is saying. I always knew books were special, wonderful worlds. The more I think about it, the more I believe it to be true.

I cast my gaze to the Monsters guarding the door and shiver. Their eyes are glowing green, and they are definitely not on the same level as Thrace.

"That is what we are trying to discover. We are looking for something. A magickal object."

"What is it?"

"If I knew that, we wouldn't still be looking," he says reasonably.

"How will you know when you find it?"

"We'll know," he states.

"Can I help?" I ask, licking my lips and hoping he doesn't see through my plan to escape.

"No," one of the twins growls.

I flick my gaze to him before I ignore him and concentrate on Thrace's blue eyes again. "Let me go?" I ask carefully.

"Are you going to run?" he asks.

"Probably," I say, unable to lie. My cheeks would give me away.

He snorts. "Honest. I like that. We are going to tear this town apart, Kate, to find what we are looking for. If you get in the way, that will include you," he says, his soothing voice turning ice-cold.

"I w-won't," I stutter quietly.

There is a silence that borders on uncomfortable as he deliberates.

"Let her go," one of the twin Monsters finally says. "That way if she runs, we can taste her blood."

I gulp and suddenly hope Thrace keeps me where I am.

"Thrasher," he snaps. "Quiet."

Thrasher – it appears his name is now – growls at him before he flicks his gaze back to me. "Tasty Kate," he almost purrs at me.

Ice slides down my spine, but I lift my chin. The heroine in the book didn't show her fear, I won't either. "What's your twin's name?" I ask boldly, needing to get my facts straight because the book is incorrect.

"Dainn," he says.

I nod, pressing my lips together. "Let me help you find what you're looking for."

"You won't know it if you see it," Thrace says, shaking his head, extending his tentacles towards me again. This time I don't flinch, and I definitely don't pass out. He strokes my face and then curls one around the back of my neck before he drags me closer to him, the chair scraping on the linoleum floor.

"I don't want to hurt you, Kate, but I will if you betray us," he whispers.

"Understood," I whisper back and make a mental note to find their way back, keep it to myself and then figure out how in the blazes to send them home without them killing me, or anyone else in this town first.

Four

Thrace

MY STEADY GAZE roves over Kate Lee, Mistress of the Book. She has absolutely no idea what she has created, nor what she is capable of. I can tell just by looking at her that she is shy and vulnerable and a little repressed. There is a part of her that is aching to be set free, but she keeps it tied up behind her prim clothes and fake pearls. I want nothing more than to pull the tie out of her ponytail and run my hands through her hair as it tumbles down around her shoulders.

She also has no idea that the reason I want to get back home so desperately is so that I can take her with me. With *us*. It's where she belongs now. She belongs to us in a way that she cannot comprehend right now. I want to show her. I want to wrap my tentacles around her and show her exactly what she means to me.

But she isn't ready.

Until she accepts who she is, we cannot go back, and we cannot claim her.

Her cheeks go red as I stare intently at her.

"What?" she stammers.

"You are very beautiful, Kate. I hope you know that," I say earnestly.

"Uhm," she mutters and looks down.

Oh, I can't wait to undo that straitlaced persona she presents to the world. I release my hold on her and see her let out a breath. She is still afraid, even though she is trying to be brave.

Waving my tentacles around her back, I undo the ties that were tying her to the chair. "You are free to leave," I murmur. "In fact, it would be preferable."

"I will help you find what you are looking for," she says.

I shake my head. "Get your bag and go home, Kate. We will see you again soon."

She realizes that she has no choice in the matter and stands up. She walks hesitantly to the door that the twins are still guarding.

They step aside to let her pass but not before Thrasher sniffs at her hair, making her jump.

Dainn, also closes in behind her and she squeaks, darting out of the door, but then lets out a shriek at a decibel that hurts my ears.

"Ah!" she screams. "What the fuck is that?"

I peer over her shoulder. "That would be Eerie," I comment. "He won't hurt you."

"Eeeeeeee," she squeals, when the giant black demon dog sniffs her face and then licks her with his rough tongue. He grazes her milky white skin. She muffles her moan of pain. "Where did he come from?" she asks through gritted teeth. "He isn't in the book."

"He's in the sequel," I inform her. "So he's in the background. Think of us as actors, Kate. The book is our movie, but we are not the characters."

"Mm-hmmm," she murmurs loudly, but is interrupted by

the low howl of Eerie shifting to his human form. He is tall and naked in front of her. Her eyes are wide as she takes in his black hair and green eyes, and I find immense delight in the fact that she can't keep her gaze from dropping to his semi hard cock. It's huge, and he can do things with it that will make you weep for mercy. I look forward to seeing him make her beg for more.

She then scampers around Eerie to the counter, where she grabs her bag and makes a run for it out of the door.

I wish she didn't have to leave, but she would get in our way here, while we tear this place apart. She loves the books too much to see the library ransacked.

Turning to Thrasher and Dainn, I snap, "Find that fucking key so we can get out of here. We don't belong and we will end up causing mayhem."

"She doesn't even know that she is supposed to come back with us," Dainn says. "That much is obvious."

"Once we find the key, the rest will fall into place, now go," I instruct and watch them disappear around the stacks and start flipping books out one by one.

Eerie strides over to me and bends from his considerable height to kiss me firmly on the lips. I push my tongue into his mouth when he grips the back of my head.

"She is skittish," he growls the obvious. "She won't come around easily."

"She will once we give her what she is crying out for," I respond confidently. "To us, she is the most beautiful woman in the world, but she doesn't see it. Once we make her feel it and she is secure, she will come to us willingly."

"And if not?" he asks.

"Then we take her back to our world by force, but that is not the preferred option, obviously."

"Humph," he mutters and with a big stretch of his arms

above his head, he turns and follows the twins to the stacks to search for the key that will open up our world and send us home, where I can then make sure that we are never disturbed again by another by destroying the key once and for all.

Five

Kate

AFTER RUNNING HOME, the instinct to hide kicks in. I lock the door and bolt it, even though that isn't going to stop any of those *Monsters* from finding me. I tried to act nonchalant about it, but Oh! My! God!

What the fucking hell was that?

Taking a moment to pinch myself to see if this is a nightmare I will wake up from, all I get is a sore arm. I gulp and back away from the door, crashing into the side table where I put my keys and mail. I drop my bag onto it and then just stand there staring at the door as if it is about to burst open and let the Monsters in.

After about five minutes, when the door *doesn't* burst open, I start to relax a little bit. Whatever they are searching for has them occupied for now, but I hope they don't hurt anyone while they are looking for it.

Shaking my head that I'm actually treating this like a normal day and that these are just normal goings-on, I head to the kitchen for a glass of water. That's when I hear a shriek from outside. I race to the front door and dare to peek out of the little window next to it, pushing the small curtain aside to peer out.

My blood runs cold when I see the giant black dog from earlier in the library. He is lumbering down the road, sniffing wildly, scaring a passer-by, when he stops, and his head turns slowly my way. I gulp and let the curtain drop, but I know those glowing green eyes saw me.

I don't move a muscle.

With my heart hammering in my chest, I freeze and then jump out of my skin when there is a knock at the door. I go lightheaded with the anxiety of the situation. What am I supposed to do? Answer it?

Licking my lips in nervousness, it's the only movement, the only sound until a deep male voice calls out, "I know you're there, Kate. I can smell you."

I nearly pee myself with the stress this is causing, hoping he means in a doggy sense and not that I stink or anything.

Debating for a few seconds on what to do, he speaks again. "Please open the door. I'm not going to hurt you."

"You would say that though, wouldn't you?" I ask.

He chuckles. "Probably, but I really am not. You are special to us, you are to be cherished, not harmed."

"Why?" I choke out.

"You will figure that out for yourself," he says.

A few more seconds pass. "I'm naked out here," he says. "Your neighbors will be wondering what's going on..." The smile in his tone makes me giggle. I can imagine the elderly couple next door with their curtains twitching.

Slowly, I reach out and slide the bolt back and then unlock the door, opening it a crack to discover that the gorgeous male is indeed naked and just as aroused as he was earlier. I'm guessing the shift does that to him. Unless he is constantly turned on, which must be hard work.

"Hi," he says. "Can I come in?"

"Fine," I say, pushing the door open and stepping back. "But if you kill me, I will come back and haunt you."

"You would make a sexy ghost," he says, taking a step forward and then over the threshold before he slams the door behind him.

"What are you doing here?" I ask. "Shouldn't you be looking for something?"

"I'd rather be here with you," he says, stepping into my personal space which makes me back up until I hit the damned side table again. He follows me and I duck around him.

"Stay over there," I demand, putting my hand up. "Or get dressed."

"I don't have any clothes," he comments. "You don't like what you see?"

I can't help raking my gaze over his hot body. "Oh, no, I like," I mutter, my cheeks going hot.

His gaze smolders when it locks onto mine. I can't keep it up and have to lower mine almost instantly. He takes a step towards me, and I stumble back, hitting the wall now. He reaches out and grasps my chin lightly in his big hand. He lifts my head up. "Don't be shy, Kate. Look at me. I want you to look, I want you to love what you see."

To my surprise, he drops to his knees in front of me and to my utter mortification, he sniffs in between my legs, letting out a feral moan when he grabs my hips. He takes my blouse in between his teeth and drags it out of the waist of my black trousers.

Still as a statue, I have no idea what to do next.

"You aren't a virgin, are you, Kate?" he murmurs.

I shake my head.

"Do you want me to touch you?"

"Get off her, you pig. Tell him, no, Kate," a sharp voice resounds around the house.

I look over Eerie's shoulder to see that Thrace has appeared in the doorway and just decided to come in.

"Apologies," he says, "I was tracking *him*. Tell him to stop and he will."

I contemplate that for a moment. I'm not sure I want him to stop. It's been a really long time since a man had his hands on me. Before my parents died, I had a serious boyfriend, but when I locked myself away, he too disappeared with my friends. I haven't dared to open up my heart again in that way since. Another thing has also dawned on me. I am pretty sure that this isn't real. It's all in my head. I think I'm trapped in my own subconscious. I'm probably still in the mental institution after a breakdown I had years ago. I was only there for six months when I was eighteen, or was I? I'm starting to think I'm still there. That this life I've built is all in my head. I mean...Monsters! Come the fuck on. They aren't real, they certainly don't appear out of books for no good reason, and they don't come after me to try and have sex with me in my small entrance hall.

Yeah, definitely, not real.

Also a small part of me knows that if I'm in this mental hell, then my parents are still alive.

It makes it easier to feel liberated. It makes it easier to just...*feel*.

"No," I say, quietly. "Don't stop."

I enjoy the low growl of satisfaction from Eerie as he flicks open the button at the side of my black pants and lowers the zipper.

They slide down my thighs and his nose goes back in between my legs to inhale deeply. Only this time, I don't shy away from it. I embrace it. I reach out and run my hand into his hair, pushing his head closer to me. He darts his tongue out and licks me through the fabric of my black cotton panties. I shiver and then gasp when Thrace sends one of his tentacles creeping around my waist to yank me away from Eerie and closer to him.

"You don't need to do this. Don't let him sway you," he murmurs.

"He isn't," I say, my head feeling foggy and like it's full of cotton wool. "I want him to touch me. I want you to touch me."

He snaps his fingers and seconds later the twins arrive, having appeared in a puff of smoke. "What about them?" Thrace asks. "Do you want them to fuck you, Kate?"

I take in their appearance again, this time with a more lustful eye. They are frightening, but that just makes it even more dangerous. Their light brown skin is rough, and their hands end in claws. Their tails swish around, with a flat disc on the end in the shape of a card's club. The horns extend from their heads and their teeth are wickedly sharp, but none of it scares me or turns me off.

"Yes," I purr. "I want you all to fuck me."

Okay, so those words came straight from the heroine in the book. But so what? It's the truth. Thrace's tentacles hook into the sides of my panties, and he pulls them down as Eerie stands up and strides over to undo my blouse. I step out of my pants and underwear, being held steady by Thrace, but then he wraps two of his tentacles around my wrists, pulling my arms out to the sides. The other three snake their way down my body, feeling every inch of my naked skin. There isn't a single thought to pull away.

The little suckers attach themselves over my nipples, drawing them into hard peaks as Eerie falls to his knees again and licks my bare slit before he wiggles his tongue against my clit, making me moan.

"Yes," I pant, wanting more. Needing more. This feels like nothing I've ever felt before, I'm craving their touch.

"Upstairs," Thrace murmurs, letting me go and then picking me up in his human arms to carry me to my bedroom.

When he lays me down on the bed and the twins climb on with me, their tails swishing over my stomach, over my pussy, I cry out and then I'm bound again by Thrace's Monster appendages, at my wrists and ankles, laid out naked and helpless for their taking.

Six

Kate

I WATCH in anticipation as Thrace extends his other arm and those fingers turn to tentacles as well. His right is keeping me tied up, but his left is inching closer to my pussy. Gasping when one of the tentacles brushes over me, I feel my clit twitch in response.

Eerie growls, scenting my reaction, my arousal and climbs on the bed as well, burying his face in between my legs to suck my clit into his mouth, his hands going under my thighs and over to hold me still.

"Oh, yes," I cry out when I can already feel the climax building. I know it's going to be a dam bursting its banks, and I can't wait. But at the same time, I don't want it to come. I want to be kept on the edge of it, waiting for it to crash over me. Eerie stops sucking my clit and shoves his tongue into me instead, while Thrace's tentacle glides over my clit, rubbing it gently. I moan and writhe on the bed, knowing the orgasm is coming and there is nothing I can do to stop it.

"Ah!" I cry out when it thunders over me, making my legs shake. All the blood has left my head, making me go dizzy.

Eerie continues to tongue-fuck me in a way that I've never experienced before, although there was only that one time, and my boyfriend wasn't that into it. Thrace lets out a low growl and Eerie moves out of the way. My breath hitches when Thrace thrusts his tentacle deep inside my pussy, making me buck on the bed. I have nowhere to go because he is holding me in place and when one of the twins, I'm not sure which, bends down to take my nipple in his mouth, grinding his sharp teeth over it, I start to beg.

"Please," I moan. "Please..."

"Do you want us to stop?" Thrace asks, still thrusting his tentacle inside me while another one pays attention to my clit.

It is sensation overload, and I don't think I can handle it.

"Yes," I pant. "No...I don't know. It's too much, I...ooooh..."

I come again in a wave of pure, undiluted pleasure, soaking the tentacle inside me.

"Fuck, you are gorgeous," Eerie growls. "So innocent, yet so wild. I need you."

I want to weep from his words. He is saying all the right things, but I protest when Thrace removes his beautiful appendage from me so that Eerie can climb on top of me.

"Let me feel you soaking my cock," he purrs in my ear, covering my body with his.

"Yes," I rasp and then squeak when he grabs my hips and at the same time as Thrace releases his hold on me, Eerie falls back to the bed, so that I'm on top. That leaves room for the twins to descend on me again, cupping my breasts and taking a nipple in their mouths to suck and bite.

"I want to taste you," one of them says. I figure this one is Thrasher because he said the same in the library.

I nod, not even having to think about it. He bites down on

my neck, his sharp teeth penetrating my flesh as Eerie lifts me up gently and then impales me on his enormous, engorged cock, filling me up and making me choke back a noise of unfettered arousal.

"Ride me, Kate," he murmurs, hands still on my hips.

I start to rock my hips, gasping when the movement causes him to rub against my g-spot. "Oh, fuck," I cry out, my hand going to the back of Thrasher's head to hold him close as he drinks my blood.

My poor brain can't comprehend what is happening right now, so I try not to think about it and just do it. Thrasher bites down harder. I scream, but take it. I don't want to push him away. My head goes woozy, and I stop moving, which causes Eerie to growl in protest.

"Enough," Thrace says, inserting his fingers between my neck and Thrasher's mouth, forcing him to release me.

Feeling the blood trickle down my skin, hot and sticky, I moan and let Dainn lean over to lap it up.

Eerie, grips my hips tighter and lifts me up slightly so that he can fuck me, thrusting deep inside me as I sit still.

"Good girl," he pants. "Stay perfectly still like a good little girl."

"Uhhh," I pant and then unexpectedly shudder as the climax smashes into me out of the blue. My pussy squeezes around Eerie's huge cock, which in turn makes him pant harder.

"Oh, yes, Kate," he murmurs. "More."

Convulsing wildly on top of him, I gasp when the tip of Dainn's tail flicks in between us and he places it on my clit, rotating it in a little circle that drives me crazy.

Crazier than I know I already am.

There is no way this can be real.

It's all in my head. I'm making it up, but I don't care. It feels fucking fantastic and I want more, so much more.

When Thrasher's bloodstained mouth lands on mine, I don't hesitate to open up so he can twist his tongue around mine, kissing me as he rakes one of his claws down the back of my neck.

"Yes," Eerie pants, thrusting into me, harder, faster, and then he groans loudly, coming in my pussy, flooding me so much, it drips back out, sliding down the inside of my thighs. I whimper into Thrasher's mouth and when he pulls back, I gasp. Thrace has withdrawn his tentacles and one of his hands is on Eerie's chest, holding him down as he licks away the cum from my skin.

"Jeeeeesus," I whisper, watching his tongue dart out, cleaning me up. "Oh, fuck."

Thrace moves his mouth over to where Eerie's cock is still buried inside me and he flicks my clit, his tongue grazing the base of Eerie's cock. I freeze, even more than I already was.

Shooting my gaze over to Eerie, his green eyes lock on mine and fill with a raw lust. Thrasher lifts me up and off Eerie's cock, sliding it out of me for Thrace to catch in his mouth and suck him clean of cum.

"Oooh," I pant, getting beyond aroused at the sight of this Monster-on-Monster action. But then Dainn swoops in to kiss me, biting my lips, his claws digging into my scalp as he deepens the kiss. Thrasher works the tip of his tail against my clit some more until I come against it with a weak cry. I'm losing my strength, but I know they are nowhere near done with me yet.

"Give her a minute to catch her breath," Thrace murmurs, taking me away from the twins and cradling me in his arms, laying me down on the bed.

"Not fair," Thrasher growls. I know it's him now. One of his horns is slightly darker than the other, whereas Dainn's are both the same color. That doesn't even sound crazy to me, in fact, it sounds perfect and comforting that I can tell them apart.

"Eerie has had his turn, what about us?"

"Kate will tell you when she is ready," Thrace says.

"I'm ready," I say straight away, even though I think if I come again so soon, I will die. But at least I will die happy and well looked after. Plus – not real. All in my head, so death won't be permanent.

I squeal in surprise when Thrasher growls again, grabbing my ankles and dragging me down the bed. He flips me over and presses me into the bed with his big, heavy body, pushing all the wind out of my lungs.

"Ack," I cry, flailing under him, but he isn't budging. He has wedged his knee in between my legs and forced my legs apart.

"Thrasher," Thrace warns him, but he pays no attention.

My moan is muffled in the rumpled bedcovers when I feel a large cock rubbing my pussy. I crane my neck to see that Thrasher has unzipped his pants, the only item of clothing he is wearing, and pulled his cock out. My eyes go wide.

"Wait," I say, trying to get away from him. "Wait!"

"No more waiting," he says and rams his cock into me with such force I scream. Well, that should be *two* cocks. He has two cocks, which means Dainn has two cocks, so that is six cocks and I have one pussy.

But I soon realize that's not the only hole I possess.

"Oh, fuck," I scream, knowing the neighbors will be able to hear me but I don't care.

Thrasher fucks me with his two cocks stuffed into my small pussy and it is like nothing I have ever felt before.

"Oh, my God," I cry, tears of pleasure pricking my eyes.

"That good, Princess?" he pants, thrusting madly, pulling on my hips to raise me up off the bed.

I get myself onto all fours so he can fuck me like an animal, slamming into me from behind.

"Yes," I pant. "Yes."

Dainn joins in, his tail sweeping underneath me, pressing the flat side against my clit, and rubbing quickly. It makes me come again, my elbows and knees shaking with the effort. Thrasher withdraws from me so that his twin can replace him, inserting his two cocks deep inside me and riding me like it's our last day on earth. Thrasher kneels next to me and jerks off, finishing off with a loud grunt and spraying his cum onto my back as his brother fucks me harder and harder until I think I'm going to pass out.

Dainn shoots his load into me a few moments later and then without even given time to take my next breath, Dainn withdraws, and Thrace pushes me over onto my back before he claims my body as the others have. His cock is out of this world. It has tiny suckers on it, like his tentacles, which rub the inside of my pussy in all the right places. I arch my back as he rides me from his position kneeling in between my legs. He has stripped naked, and his body is droolworthy, like the others.

What do they see in me?

I'm plain and boring.

Do they just want me because I'm clearly a pushover when it comes to having filthy, dirty sex with them?

That thought sits uneasily on me until Thrace falls on top of me and kisses me sweetly, still pounding into me. "Don't think those nasty thoughts, Kate. We want you because you are ours."

"How did you know...?" I ask, but the thought gets lost in the wave of ecstasy that pulsates through me and finishes me off completely as Thrace joins me over the cliff edge of deep lust.

I simply cannot move another inch.

"We have worn you out," Thrace murmurs, pressing his mouth over the bite wound and soothing it with his tongue. "We should've been more careful with you."

"No," I say with a smile as he tucks me in. "I loved it."

"We did too," Eerie says, stroking my face. "We will leave you to sleep, dear Kate."

I nod sleepily, and my eyes have closed before they have even left the room.

Seven

Eerie

I AM reluctant to leave her.

She is sleeping and vulnerable. I want to shift and snuggle up next to her, not only for reassurance that she will be safe, but for my own needs. The attachment bond has formed quickly and is stronger than anything I have ever known. She is mine. There isn't a single thing I wouldn't do for her, not a single being I wouldn't kill to protect her.

Being in the book has been dark and lonely, and while it has been our place while we sought out the Mistress of the Book to release us from that prison, it has not been a pleasant experience. We were destined from the second we were printed on the pages of the magickal book to come to life and live out the fantasy that was not ours.

Now it is our turn. Once we find the key, we can go back home and lock ourselves away in the life that *we* want. That we require. Our sole purpose for coming here was to capture Kate and to bring her home.

But taking her by force is not the way we want to do this. We want her to *want* to come with us. It makes all the difference in the world.

"Eerie, come now. You need to leave her to rest. We have given her too much of ourselves. It was wrong," Thrace murmurs.

"Being inside her was not wrong," Thrasher mutters on my behalf. "It was very right, and it was where we belong."

"She is in a delicate state," he says, whisking us back to the library with his magick puff of smoke. "She believes we aren't real. She believes she has imagined us and that we only want her because she has allowed us to claim her body in the way that we have. Her thoughts are..." He pauses, a concerned look on his face.

"Are what?" I ask with a frown.

"Disturbing," he says shortly. "She is unable to see that we want her for her, or even that we are real."

"Then we make her see," Dainn growls.

"No, that is exactly what we don't want. We don't want to scare her off. She needs to be handled with care and consideration. She has suffered a trauma that has caused her to retreat from the world."

"It isn't fair that you get to see into her mind, and the rest of us don't," I grumble petulantly.

"It is not a gift," he says sharply. "Not when she is so unhappy."

"We can bring her joy," I say. "Why can't we just tell her?"

"Because then it won't be her choice. We agreed the night we came here, that she brought us here, that we would let it be her choice."

Sighing with frustration, I turn from him. "I need to eat something. I'm going to find someone to kill," I growl and without waiting for an answer, I shift into my demon dog form and stalk towards the front doors of the library, nudging them open and then prowling outside on the hunt for food. The incredible sex has made me ravenous. I have half a mind to eat and then go back to Kate's, but Thrace would be super pissed at me if I did. Not that it usually bothers me because, let's face it, he is an enormous stick-in-the-mud. Always pious and doing the right thing. Always telling us off for following our darker instinct.

However, right now he has insight into Kate's mind, the fucker, and he will withhold information if I do anything to piss him off. He can also be incredibly petty.

I find it amusing most days, as only a lover can, but seriously, taking a step back and knowing how I feel about Kate now, yeah, I can see his faults quite clearly.

I growl, low and deep in my throat and lumber forward, surprising the man coming around the corner of this quiet street, walking his dog. He yells and backs up, the dog starts barking, but at one look from me, it quietens down to a whimper. The man turns to run, but I open up my mouth, venomous drool dripping from my fangs and bite down over his head, shutting him up and killing him in one fell swoop. His bones crack and his blood gushes into my mouth. I chomp him into little bits, relishing the taste and swallowing with satisfaction.

"Tasty," Thrasher says, strolling up behind me. "Wish you'd saved some for me."

I curl my lip up and growl. I don't share food. He knows this by now.

"Are you going back to Kate's?" he asks casually.

I huff and turn from him.

"You took a risk going to her earlier. It paid off, but it was still a risk," he continues. "You should probably leave her alone for a bit. She took us all without complaint, but we definitely wore her out."

The fact that she doesn't think we are real, hits me in the

chest suddenly and it hurts. I whimper and drop my head before I shift and let out a loud moan.

"Hurts me too," Thrace says, appearing behind me. "But we have to do what's best for her."

I let him come to me and wrap his arms around me. He has the comfort thing down to a tee and my frustration at his gift dissipates.

"Come back to the library, we will keep searching. It was supposed to be with the book, but the book is on the shelf without the key. Where the fuck is it?" he mutters.

I shrug. I don't feel like talking now. Or searching. All I want to do is curl up next to Kate and sleep with her. My dick has gone hard again as well and needs some attention.

Thrace notices and says, "Let me take care of that for you."

I nod as he leads me back inside and closes the library doors behind us. As Thrasher goes back to searching with Dainn, Thrace takes my hand, and we disappear into the back office. He drops to his knees and takes my cock in his mouth. I close my eyes and drop my head back as he sucks me off hard and fast, just the way I like it.

I groan and place my hand on the back of his head, pushing his mouth further onto me until he is deep throating me.

Thinking of Kate makes me come in his mouth, spurting my hot load down his throat, which he swallows and then stands up to kiss me.

I wrap my hand around his throat and squeeze tightly. "Don't keep anything from me," I whisper. "If she thinks about sneezing, I want to know about it."

He sends a tentacle up to wrap around my wrist and pulls my hand away. "Of course," he says with just a hint of smugness that makes me wonder if he will.

Something tells me he is going to keep all of her thoughts to himself to give himself the advantage.

He must know that will piss me off, and he knows how I react when I'm pissed off. This world isn't ready for it.

Eight

Kate

I AWAKE from a deep slumber and stretch. Groaning, I
ache from head to toe, especially between my legs. I have never
been cock-battered like that before. It's any wonder I'm still
alive after it.

Swinging my legs over the side of the bed, I stand up
unsteadily and hobble to the bathroom. Sitting down to pee, I
squeal with the burn and then decide without a doubt, it's
time for a shower before anything else. I climb in and blast the
water as hot as I can bear it to ease my aching muscles, placing
a warm damp washcloth between my legs.

Several minutes later, feeling less sore and more refreshed,
I turn the water off and grab a towel from the rack. Then I
scream my head off when I see Thrace sitting on the closed
toilet, his legs crossed at the knee.

"Morning," he says, rising gracefully and picking up the
towel I dropped. He holds it out and wraps it around me,

drawing me closer until I'm pressed up against him. "How do you feel this morning?"

"Sore," I grumble.

He chuckles softly. "Oh, my precious girl. You will get used to us. Next time we will be gentler with you."

"Please," I murmur. My cheeks go hot when I realize that I've just told him I want them to ravage me again.

"Coffee?" he asks, stepping away and giving me my personal space back.

I nod and watch him disappear to the kitchen. Taking the opportunity to hurriedly get dry and dressed, I'm fully clothed in my usual attire of black pants with a white blouse when he returns.

"You look lovely," he says, handing me a steaming mug.

"You're a liar, but thanks, anyway."

"No lies, Kate. You are the most beautiful woman. I adore you. We all do. Please believe us."

"Mm." I take a sip of coffee, grateful to be hiding my face from him. "What brings you by?" I ask after I swallow. It doesn't even bother me that he has used his Monster power to enter my home without permission. I mean, not real, right, so who cares?

Deep down though, I'm starting to not buy that excuse as much. I want to because then all of this makes sense, but if the last few years have all been in my head, then why would I kill my own parents and cause myself so much grief? I wouldn't. So if that is real, then this has to be as well.

Doesn't it?

I push it aside to deal with at another time.

"I just wanted to check on you after yesterday," he says, having a look around my bedroom, almost as if he is expecting to find something.

"I'm okay."

His gaze lasers in on mine. "Are you?"

I nod. "Are you okay?"

He snickers. "I'm great. I more than enjoyed our time together. I'm eager to do it again. So are the others."

He steps into my personal space again and my heart thumps in my chest. I look up and lick my lips nervously. "Have you found the thing you were looking for?"

"Not yet," he clips out in an annoyed tone. His eyes turn stormy, and I wish I hadn't mentioned it. The air of menace that is emanating from him has made the hairs on the back of my neck stand on end.

"I—I can help you look," I stammer, just to try and ease the discomfort of the situation.

"No need. We will find it in good time. Are you going to the library today?"

"Yes."

"I will walk you."

"Uhm...are the others still there?" I ask tentatively.

"We have exhausted our search of the library. We will be moving on," he replies.

"I really want to help..."

"Trying to get rid of us?" he asks, those blue eyes burning with a challenge.

"Not at all, but it seems important."

He narrows his eyes and purses his lips. "It is," he says and leaves it at that.

He possessively takes my elbow and leads me out of the bedroom and downstairs. He releases me to collect my belongings and then he takes my hand and ushers me out of the front door.

"No smoky magick transportation?" I murmur.

"Not today. I want to enjoy this stroll with you before the others get their hands on you again."

The shiver of delight that passes over me, thrills me. No

one has ever treated me like I'm something to treasure before. I could get used to this.

Once again, I notice that there aren't many people about. Life isn't going on as normal, which is just another nail in the theory that this is really real, and I'm currently being escorted by a tentacle-wielding Monster to my place of work.

"Where is everyone?" I mutter, not realizing I said it out loud.

"You are concerned about someone in particular?" he growls.

I shake my head, noticing the flash of jealousy on his face before it passes.

Something is definitely not right here, and I don't just mean about the Monsters prowling around and fucking me every which way, including sideways.

Where the fuck are all the townspeople?

Nine

Thrasher

SUCKING the marrow out of the thigh bone of the human I just ate, I lick my lips in satisfaction.

"Are you finished?" Dainn asks exasperated.

"For now," I remark, looking around the small park area. There are hardly any people walking around. They must've spotted us and are staying indoors away from us. Not that it will save them. If we're hungry, we eat. Plain and simple.

"Good. Now go look under that bush," Eerie snaps at me. "We have wasted too much time looking for this damn key. I want to go back to our world with Kate."

"I want the same thing, asshole," I growl, ready for the fight he is clearly angling for. I hold my hand up, flashing my claws at him and then curl my fingers in, one by one in a dramatic gesture that has Dainn snickering.

"Quit bitching, both of you," he grouses. "There is fuck all here. Let's move on."

We turn as one to head over the road to the playground

with swings and a slide for small humans. I narrow my eyes, catching sight of something slinking under the slide.

"Wait," I say, holding up my hand. "There's something over there."

"A human?" Dainn asks, his stomach grumbling with hunger.

I don't share food. He wants something to eat, he has to find it himself.

"No," I say, drawing Eerie closer.

"What then?"

"One of us," I mutter and cross over the road with long strides, making short work of the distance.

"Us?" Dainn asks. "We are all here."

I roll my eyes at him. He isn't the sharpest tool in the shed. "I don't mean *us*, I mean a Monster like us. A serpent..."

"Where?" Eerie asks, joining me and peering under the slide. "I don't see anything."

"It was there, I swear I saw it," I say, also bending down. "Is it possible we brought something else with us out of our world?"

"How? And we don't have a Serpent Monster in our world."

I shrug. "I don't know then. But I know what I saw." Well, kind of. I'm not admitting to anyone now that I might've been wrong. Fuck that. I'm sticking to my story come hell or high water, stubborn ass that I am. At least I know my faults.

"Humph," Eerie says and then straightens up. "Fuck this. I want to find Kate. And where the fuck is Thrace?"

"Right here," he says, appearing in that way cool puff of smoke thing he does. "Did you find it?"

"Not yet," I reply. "But we found something else."

"No, we didn't," Eerie interrupts. "You thought you saw a Serpent Monster, but it's disappeared."

"A Serpent?" Thrace asks, his brow creasing. "Where did it come from?"

"Good question," I ask. "Any ideas?"

Thrace shakes his head, but his eyes are narrowed and that means he's thinking. He knows or has an idea; he just doesn't want to share.

"Where were you?" Eerie barks at him.

"With Kate. I escorted her to work."

Eerie lets out a low growl. "Without us?"

"I wanted to check on her and then I walked her to work. Nothing happened," Thrace says blandly.

"You are such a dick," I inform him. "Sneaking in there while we do all the searching. It's time you got your hands dirty for a change."

"I have been searching," he replies. "So fuck you, Thrasher."

I snarl and move in, ready to wipe that imperious look off his face. I lash out with my tail, but his tentacles come out and hold me at bay.

"Don't," he says quietly. "I will beat you and you know it."

I let out a low rumble from deep inside and whip my tail out of his grasp. I do know it and he will never let anyone forget that he could wipe the floor with our faces if he chose to. It pisses me off. I'm no lightweight. It's why I'm here. It's why the four of us are here, to bring the Queen home with us. But for the love of fuck, the key has gone missing. We can't get back without it.

It unsettles me and makes me even more aggressive than I would normally try to be. Dainn is the impulsive, feral one. I try to keep a more rational head to make up for his lack of thought. It's been that way for as long as I can remember. Although, having said that, I have no clue how long that really is.

Our memories are implanted, up until the point of us coming here. Only Thrace seems to know what's gone on in the past with any certainty. It doesn't usually bother me, but today I find it irritating, but that is because I'm frustrated. I need to be near Kate. She brings a sense of calm with her complete lack of fear of us. Yes, when she first saw us, she was terrified, but that has changed. Thrace says it's because she thinks we are all in her head. I want to show her that we are real, mean her no harm, and that we are here to love and worship her. She is our everything and will bring our world to life once we return there. Being here in this place doesn't sit well with me. All I want to do is smash and destroy and kill.

"What is it?" Eerie asks, shoving me to bring me back to the present.

"Nothing. Just want out of here."

"Same," he says. "Keep hold of that viciousness a little while longer. To tear this place apart before we are ready to leave isn't in our best interests."

"I know. I'm trying. When can we see Kate again?"

"Later," Thrace snaps at me. "Get back to looking. And if you see that Serpent Monster again, pin it to the ground and find out where the fuck it came from."

I nod, hoping that we find it so I can do a bit of maiming before the day is out.

Ten

Kate

STARING out over the quiet library, I wonder again where everyone is. Sandy is a no-show and when I tried to call her, she didn't pick up. Something weird is going on. I wonder if instead of the Monsters being in my world, I'm suddenly in the book world.

I jump when the door to the library opens and in walks Doris, squashing that theory good and dead.

"Morning!" she calls out. "Did Hell's Belle by that Eve Newton woman come in yet? I want a piece of that sexy Monster action!"

I fluster. Normally I would know the answer to that, but my head is so far up my own ass this morning, I don't know. "I'll just check," I call back and bend down under the counter to see if her latest sexy tome has arrived in the box today from the neighboring town's library.

"Yes!" I exclaim, pulling it out and standing up, only to shriek my head off when I'm confronted not with Doris, but with a gigantic snake looking creature.

"Ahhhhhhhh!" I shout, holding the book up in front of me as if that's going to help.

It hisses, towering over me, its forked tongue flicking in and out, tasting the air.

"Holy mother of fuck!" Doris yells.

I find myself relieved that the old woman is still here and did not turn into the huge snake Monster thing.

She skirts around the snake, coming up to me behind the counter. It only just notices her, and bends down to hiss in our faces as we just stand there completely frozen.

"Eeeeeeeeeee," I squeal, turning my head to the side as its tongue darts out and it bares fangs so huge, they look like tusks with venom dripping from them.

"Where the fucking hell did that come from?" Doris whispers in my ear.

"Shhhhhhhh," I mutter and push her carefully behind me as we take a step back. But there isn't much space behind the counter. We are trapped.

The only good thing about this situation is that Doris can also see it. I'm not hallucinating or delusional. It must've come out of the book with the others, but I don't remember it.

"Make a run for it, towards the fire exit at the back of the thriller section," I murmur out of the side of my mouth to Doris.

"Okay," she stage whispers back and we sidle slowly to the side.

The snake's glowing green eyes follow us, its tongue still flicking in and out.

When the counter ends and there's nothing in between it and us, I grab Doris's hand and we launch ourselves towards the back of the library, me a lot faster than her, but practically dragging her along with me.

The snake lets out something between a roar and a hiss,

and slithers after us so fast, it catches us and corners us within seconds.

"Ahhh!" I scream again and then nearly faint with relief when Thrace smokes into view, tentacles waving, fury on his face as he faces off with the snake.

"Ours!" he bellows and whips a tentacle around the snake, hoisting it off the ground and waving it in the air.

"Hooooly shit," Doris mutters, mouth agape as she stares at the scene in front of her.

I wonder how in the hell I'm supposed to explain this to her.

Still gripping her hand, I lead her slowly and carefully around the stacks so we can peek out from behind the safety of them to see what Thrace is doing to the snake.

"Get. Out!" Thrace bellows, and it takes me a second to realize he is talking to me.

Pulling Doris along, we skirt around to the office, and I let go of her hand to open the big window that leads to freedom.

I climb out first and then lean back in to help the old woman out. She is pretty spry though, and doesn't need much assistance.

We collapse in a heap on the grass as she grips my arms and falls forward. "Kate," she says calmly. "What is going on?"

I stand up, brushing off my pants. Helping her rise, I lead her to a nearby bench in the shelter of a few trees. Although, thinking about it, some snakes live in trees. I glance up with caution and then decide to sit out in the open where we might see something coming.

"I don't know," I say quietly, once we are seated and have our breath back. I lean forward and rest my head on my hands, my elbows propped up on my knees. "Doris, you've known me a long time. You knew my parents. You know how much I loved them."

"Of course I do, dear," she says, patting my leg.

"I thought...I saw these Monsters a few days ago, and I thought they were in my head. I thought I'd made them up. But then I realized that my parents were still dead, and I wouldn't do that, even in my head. My dreams consist of them still being alive. So maybe, just maybe this is all real. That I recovered from my mental breakdown, and this is actually all happening. I wouldn't do that, would I, Doris? I wouldn't still have my parents dead if this was all in my head?"

She blows out a breath before she speaks. "I can't answer that, love," she says eventually. "I can only imagine that you wouldn't. But I know I'm real and those...things in there..." She gestures towards the library in the short distance. "I saw them."

"So it's real," I murmur. "How? How did any of this happen?"

"What do they want?" she asks. "Do you know?"

I have to love how rational she is being about this and not freaking the fuck out like I'm on the verge of. Everything I've said and done to them, I wouldn't have if I knew they were *real*. I mean, the...sex. Fuck, you can't even call it that. It was more than that, it was like something out of a fantasy, out of a *book*. I can't tell Doris that they seem to want *me*. What if she turns around and offers me to them in exchange for her life? I give her a sketchy glare, but then hate myself for thinking such a horrible thing of the sweet woman who has been nothing but kind to me.

"They're after something to send them back to the book world," I mutter.

"Book world?" she muses, then snaps her fingers. "I thought I recognized that tentacle guy!"

I shudder. She's read the same book as me? Gross, gross, gross.

"So they appeared and now they want to go back, but need this thing, this key?"

49

"Yeah." All of a sudden, it's like a lightning bolt has struck. "Key," I mutter under my breath. I had forgotten all about the old-fashioned key I found in the safe on top of the book. How did I forget it after all the talk about them finding something to send them home? It's in my bag...the bag that is currently on top of the counter in the library that houses a snake Monster fighting with a tentacle Monster.

Great, just great.

Eleven

Thrace

Now that I know Kate is safe, I loosen my hold on the Serpent, but I don't let go.

"Stay away from her. She is mine," I inform it.

"Ourssssssss," it hisses. "We want the book goddesssssss."

"Nope, told you, she is mine. You aren't going near her..."

Its tongue darts out, flicking menacingly at me, but I'm not scared of this thing. There are few creatures who can defeat the real me.

"Where did you even come from?" I ask it curiously.

"Helllll," it snarls.

I roll my eyes at it. "Yeah, okay, pal. Listen up. Stay away from Kate or I will eat you alive."

"You can't do that," it sneers, its green eyes lighting up with amusement.

"No?" With a low growl, I let my full Monster out to show this Serpent that he went after the wrong girl. I grow several feet taller; my tentacles grow longer and wider and then my body shifts into that of the Kraken.

The Serpent hisses and spits, but it is useless. I have it in my grip and I tighten it again, opening my giant maw. I lift the Serpent up even higher and then unwind the tentacle that has hold of it, so it drops into my mouth. I snap my jaws shut and devour the Serpent whole.

"Asshole," Eerie mutters, coming into my line of sight. "You really are."

Giving him a steely glare, I shift back, snapping my fingers to re-clothe myself with the magick that consumes me. "It was going after Kate," I inform him.

"You realize that it belonged to another book world. Now what?"

I shrug, unconcerned. "That is nothing that worries me. Getting back to our world with Kate, is."

"Begs the question, though. Did all the books come to life? Is she some sort of special creature for *all* book worlds? I thought she was just ours."

"It's interesting," I murmur and cast a glance over to where Kate and the old woman disappeared. "There is a woman with Kate. She is off limits. I don't care about anyone else in this town, but you and the boys stay away from her. She is special to Kate. Losing her will cause her unnecessary pain. Do you understand me?" My gaze pierces his and he nods, knowing that I mean business. He rarely sees me in my true form. None of them do. It's unwieldy and I can't speak to other beings that are not my kind. I only bring it out when my opponent needs to be taught not to mess with me and that Serpent was a vicious pest who did not know how to back away from a fight it couldn't win. It would've annoyed the shit out of me. My telepathic ability seems to have extended to wrap around Kate's thoughts and I have no doubt that when we have bonded properly over time, she will be able to communicate with me the same way. It thrills me and makes me hard just for her.

"Speaking of the boys...where are they?"

"Thrasher is out hunting for that thing you just ate. It got a bug up his ass for some reason. Dainn is looking for food."

"Go now and tell them what I've ordered. The woman remains unharmed."

"Of course," Eerie says and slopes off into the shadows to do as I've asked.

I follow Kate's footsteps and cross over into the office to see the window wide open. I stick my head out and see the two women talking on a bench a little way away. I squint and focus on Kate. She is uncertain, but something has shifted in her. Something deep and it terrifies me.

It makes my cold blood turn to ice.

She is afraid. Afraid of *us*.

Her gaze locks onto mine and she cowers for a moment before sitting up straighter. Her body is primed and ready to dart away.

There's no need to fear me, Kate.

She shakes her head, having heard me, but unsure how.

I want to go to her and reassure her, but that will only make her run. She has decided that we are a threat to her and that won't be easy to disprove right now. I duck back inside and close the window with a sigh. I miss her already. I can *feel* that she has pulled away from me and it is tugging on my heart. We need to increase our efforts to find the key and return to our world with her as our Queen. It is the only way she will see we mean her no harm, only care.

With a frustrated growl, I swipe everything off the desk with my extended tentacles and storm out of the office, a wave of fury following behind me as I exit the library and make my way to the center of this small town to focus and see if the key will lead me to it.

Twelve

Kate

Seeing Thrace gave me chills. I'm glad he didn't come after me. He must know that I'm more cautious now. I know he projected that thought into my head. However he does that.

"Doris," I say, standing up. "It's not safe around here. Please will you come and stay with me, so I know you're safe?"

She looks up at me and huffs. She rises as well and faces me. "I'll come and stay with you, Kate, but just to make sure *you're* safe. Something hinky is going on around here, and I promised your parents I'd look out for you if anything ever happened to them."

My heart pangs with love for them. I nod, accepting that, but only because she is determined to keep me safe, whereas I'm determined to keep her safe. Either way, she is coming home with me where I can keep an eye on her.

"Let me grab my bag from the library and then we'll swing by yours for some things," I say.

She nods and looks back at the small building. "Do you think they've gone?"

I inhale deeply. "One way to find out."

She makes a noise of agreement and silently we sneak up to the front doors of the library and peer through the glass. It's dark inside as expected. The lighting is quite dim in places.

"I can't see anything," I mutter.

"Me either," Doris confirms.

"Wait here."

"No way."

I give her a frustrated glare, but it's like water off a duck's back. So, I open the door and slip inside, not surprised when she follows me. I pause and look towards the back of the library where Thrace and the snake were, but all is quiet.

I press my finger to my lips when I glance at Doris, and we creep forward. I snatch up my bag without incident, wondering what in the name of hell happened to the snake Monster, but not so much that I want to hang around to find out.

"Get that book," Doris hisses at me.

"What?"

"Hell's Belle. I've been waiting ages to read it."

I growl at her, but bend to retrieve it from the floor where I'd dropped it when the snake Monster chased us.

Shoving it in my bag, we rush back to the front door, and I shut it, digging in my bag for the key to lock it. That's when I notice that the other key isn't there. I scrabble through the entire contents twice, but come up short of an old-fashioned iron key.

"Dammit," I mutter. Did they already find it?

"What are you looking for?" Doris whispers loudly.

"Nothing," I reply and lock the library up before looping my arm through hers and turning to walk to her house a short distance away.

My mind reeling with all of this crazy shit that's going on, it takes Doris a couple of times to get my attention.

"Mmm?" I murmur when she stops and taps me on the shoulder.

"They want *you*, don't they?" she asks.

I feel my cheeks heat up. "What makes you think that?"

"That tentacle one was protecting you from the snake. I may be an old bat, but I'm not blind or daft."

"Oh," I say, my blush deepening until I feel like my face is going to set on fire. "Maybe."

"Tell Aunty Doris what you've got yourself into," she says.

We start walking again.

"I wish I knew," I say after a hefty pause. "I thought it was all..." I tap my temple.

"Hm," she murmurs. "What do they want with you?"

I shrug. "Just me, to take me back to their world with them."

"Oooh," she chuckles. "Like that is it?"

"Stop it," I chide her. "Not like that at all."

"Yeah, right," she snorts. "I was young once. In fact, I was a bit like you, Kate. Shy and reserved and didn't know how beautiful I was. It was only when my darling Harold *showed* me that I was a catch that I believed it."

"How did he do that?" I ask, intrigued and glad the subject has been taken off me for a moment.

"We went out one night and he pointed out all the men who had their eye on me!" she cackles. "I was a curvy girl but all in the right places, like you, Kate. There was nothing short of ten men who eyed me up that night. Harold thought it was hilarious, but he was so proud to be with me. That's when I decided to take control of my life and just be who I wanted to be, instead of crawling into a hole whenever anyone spoke to me. If these...whatever they are...Monsters, I guess? If they make you feel special, why not embrace it?"

I gape at her in astonishment. "Because they are *Monsters*," I hiss.

"So?" she asks with a shrug. "Who cares?"

"Me!" I exclaim. "I care. They are dangerous and...why are we even talking about this? It's insanity. The whole town has been drugged and we are hallucinating or something...."

"Nope," Doris says. "I tried mushrooms back in the day. I don't feel out there at all."

Eyes wide, I look at her, a laugh escaping my lips. "Oh, you are a riot, you know that?" I ask, snickering uncontrollably.

"I try," she says with a delicate sniff before she also bursts out laughing.

Moments later, we stop outside her house, still giggling.

"I'll just be a minute," she says, opening the door and letting me inside.

I nod and wait, closing the door behind me. I have a look around at the hundreds of photos of her and her late husband, Harold. He was a good-looking man and sounds like one of the good ones. They never had kids, and seemed to live their best life, traveling all over and enjoying each other. I want that with someone. Someones? Some *Monsters*?

"Ready," Doris says, interrupting my thoughts.

"Let's go," I say, taking the small bag from her.

She smiles and we leave her small, cozy home to head to mine where I hope there isn't a tentacle Monster waiting to whisk me away in a puff of smoke.

Or do I?

Thirteen

Dainn

Licking the blood from my lips, I turn from the pile of bones from the human I just stripped bare and wince. My head hurts.

Too much food. Kate. Kate. Kate.

I slap my hand to my head and drop to my knees. My thoughts are racing again. Thrasher, Thrace, Eerie, they all think that I'm slow or impaired because I don't speak much and my actions are sometimes dulled, but it's because my thoughts move too quickly for the rest of me to keep up. They hound me day and night.

Kate. Kate. Home.

I want to go back home. I want to go back home to the forest where things are familiar, and it smells like home and not this weird smell that fills this land.

Home. Forest. Kate. Too full.

I groan and then my delicate nose picks up the scent of Kate. It soothes me for a moment. *She* soothes me. Being in her presence calms my thoughts, makes me able to think and act more rationally, instead of picking out the loudest thought and going with that. I hate the way my brain works. I want to be quieter in my head. I want to be able to focus on things instead of having them be a flash in the pan. Only being with Kate allows me that peace, that *choice*.

Loping over the grass, following the scent of Kate, I stop at a bench and sniff it wildly. She was here, but she's gone again.

Kate. Home. Kate. Brain too full of thoughts.

Looking up and around, I pick up her scent again and follow it. I don't care if we're not supposed to be with her unless Thrace says so. I *need* her in ways that the others don't.

Lumbering down the road, I see Kate and an old woman coming out of a house. I speed up, racing to get to her, wanting my thoughts to slow down so that I can speak to her.

Skidding to a stop in front of her, she gasps and clutches the bag she is holding tighter. I ignore the old woman. She doesn't interest me. Being with Kate is the only thing I need.

"Kate," I croak out, the relief flooding me when the peace she brings settles over me. "Please don't leave me."

"What?" she squeaks, sounding almost terrified of me.

I look deep into her eyes, and I see her fear. It makes me sad.

Sad. Sad. Kate. Home. Maim. Kill.

I scrunch my eyes shut. The calm is vanishing, sifting through my fingers like sand. She is afraid and it is affecting her ability to soothe me.

No. No. No. Please, Kate...

"Dainn!"

I turn around and see Eerie stalking towards me.

"Get away from them."

"No," I whisper. "I need Kate." I glance back at her. "Please, don't leave me, Kate."

"I—I..." She shakes her head, and grabs the old woman, skirting around me and rushing down the street.

I spin to go after them, but Eerie stops me with a hand on my arm. "Leave them be. And don't go after the old woman. She is with Kate. Thrace's orders."

"Need her," I pant as I start to drown in my thoughts again. I pull my arm from his grip, but he is determined to stop me.

He shifts to his demon dog form in a burst of fur that was lightning quick and must've hurt him. His howl of pain turns into a growl of warning. He swipes my feet out from under me and places his paw on my chest.

Struggling under the weight of him, I rake his pelt with my claws, but he is impervious to the damage they can cause.

I stop struggling as my brain races along and I try to switch off.

Kate. Need. Kate. Help. Please help.

Eerie shifts again and takes his weight off my chest. "Thrace said no. Got it?"

I nod, the action hurting my head. He glances in the direction Kate went and I curl up on the warm ground, seeking comfort.

But it doesn't come.

Darkness falls.

Coldness sweeps over me.

I ache, but I force myself to move, helped up by my twin who doesn't suffer the same affliction as me.

"Get up, we need you to help look for the key," he growls.

Key. Key. Home. Kate. Help. Kate. Need.

Grunting my response, I blink a couple of times to try and clear my head. But it's no use. Only Kate can do that when she believes in me. She doesn't anymore. What did I do to make her fear me?

Fear. Kate. Afraid. Hurts. Head. Home. Key. Need. Kate.

Closing my eyes to take away the pain, I take a deep breath.

"Dainn," Thrasher snaps at me, getting frustrated, but he doesn't understand. I have never been able to find the words to tell him that I'm wired differently.

"Coming," I mumble and follow him down the street and into someone's front garden. Thrasher kicks the door in, and I hear the people inside scream. It seems we are now increasing our efforts to find our way back home. I gaze longingly down the road where Kate disappeared and then back to the house Thrasher broke into.

There is no choice.

I turn from my twin and run down the road to Kate's house, needing her to hold me and to heal me. I don't give a flying fuck what Thrace will do to me when he finds me there.

I will take any punishment, if only she can heal my head.

Fourteen

Kate

Once I've settled Doris into the small guest room, she insists on making dinner. Who's going to refuse that offer? Not me, that's for sure. I can cook, sometimes I enjoy it, but I've been doing everything myself for years. A break would be nice.

It occurs to me belatedly that Doris has been doing everything herself as well for longer years than me. Tomorrow, I'm going to treat her to a day of complete rest.

With a smile at the thought of pampering her, I find my heart filled with a sudden love for her. I've always known her. I didn't know she was that close to my parents, but they used to stop and talk in the street or at the supermarket when we bumped into her when I was little. I guess a deeper friendship grew once I'd moved out for her to say she'd look out for me.

Blinking as something suddenly seems off about that. Why would my parents ask her to look out for me if something happened to them? How could they know that they'd be killed in a car accident? It seems...strange.

Not that I doubt Doris. She is as transparent as they come, but the heavy question of why my parents would say that is now hanging over my head.

With a sigh, I pick up my bag and empty the contents all over the coffee table. The fact that this key is missing is also a great concern to me. If I had it, I could give it back to Thrace and they could leave. Without me, of course.

I search through the entire contents, strewn across the table, but I don't find it.

"Dammit," I mutter, biting my bottom lip. "Where the hell did it go?"

"What are you looking for?" Doris asks, coming into the sitting room, wiping her hands on a towel.

"Nothing," I murmur.

"Hmm, dinner will be ready in about five minutes," she says and then looks through the items laid out in front of her. "This that key?" she asks, bending down to pick something up.

"What key?" I ask in confusion.

"The one to send them back," she says slowly, giving me a curious look.

"No, I know that, but I mean *what* key? There is no key here."

She frowns at me and waves her hand in front of my face. "This key."

I shake my head. "I don't see anything," I say, my gaze meeting hers.

Her frown deepens, and so does mine.

"You can't see it?" she asks after a beat.

"Nope. Are you sure you're holding it?" I inquire tentatively.

Her gaze turns scathing. "What did we say about me being

a blind, daft old bat? I'm not one. There is a big old key in my hand, which I can see and feel, but apparently you can't!"

"Okay, I believe you," I say quickly, standing up. I wave my hand over hers. "Am I touching it?"

"Your hand is going straight through it," she mutters. "How strange. You saw it before, though?"

I nod. "Yep. It was on top of the book, and I picked it up and put it in my bag."

"I wonder what's changed that you can't see it now, but I can..." Her gaze shoots to mine. "You don't believe, do you?"

"Believe what? In the Monsters. Oh, I know they're there," I huff.

"No, I don't mean in that way. You don't believe in *them*."

"What? And you do?" I ask incredulously.

"Why not?" she asks, "In, my, admittedly, limited experience, vicious tentacle wielding Monsters, don't protect human women from creepy snake Monsters, just for the fun of it."

Grimacing at her, I can't fault her logic, *but* that doesn't mean anything. I guess I see her point, but what unearthly magick is this, that they've come out of the world anyway and need this invisible key to return home. Can they even see it? If I can't hold it, then I have no hope of returning it to them.

A ding sounds from the kitchen and Doris says, "Dinner's ready." She replaces the unseen key in my bag, to keep it safe, presumably and then bustles off to the kitchen. I follow after her, suitably cowed. I feel like I owe her an apology for not believing these Monsters have my best interests at heart. But for all I know, they only need me to send them home.

* * *

After a beautifully made spaghetti and sauce with garlic bread, I clear up.

"Heading to bed," Doris says. "I've got some reading to do!"

I giggle at her obvious joy and wave her off. "Night, Doris. I'll have tea and breakfast ready for you in the morning."

"Oh, there's no need to do that," she says, brushing it off.

"Yes, there is. Let me take care of you for a bit."

"Oh," she says, her cheeks blushing with pleasure. "Oh, you're a good girl."

Smiling as she disappears up to bed, I hear a soft knock on the back door. I step towards it, but then freeze. There is no one around to 'drop by' and knock on the back door. All the people have vanished, except for Doris and me.

"Kate, please, open up," a rough voice says.

Dainn.

He came up to us in the street earlier asking me not to leave him. I figured it was just part of their plan, but the sadness, almost desperation in his voice now eats at my very soul. With a shaking hand and cursing my good nature, I reach for the door handle and turn it.

Opening it a crack, I see the Monster curled up on the mat. He looks up at me with adoration in his eyes and I gasp.

"Wh-what do you want?" I stammer.

"Just your permission to sleep here tonight, please. Being near you soothes the noise in my head," he says quietly.

"Ooh," I murmur, my heart hammering in my chest. I blink rapidly and nod slowly, not feeling like I can deny another living creature who is clearly in pain.

His relieved expression punches me in the heart and biting my lip, I stop thinking and act. I hold my hand out for him.

"Come inside. But you don't hurt my friend."

His surprised expression makes me smile. "I wouldn't hurt your friend, Kate, because that would hurt you," he says, getting to his feet.

I sigh. "I don't know what you really want with me, or

what you've done with everyone who lives here, but you obviously need some TLC."

He exhales slowly and takes my hand.

I lead him inside, wondering where my senses have gone, but I know in my soul he won't hurt me or Doris. He is a creature who appears to be a bit misunderstood.

I know how that feels.

Fifteen

Eerie

Not overly amused by Dainn's disappearance earlier, my nose is to the ground sniffing out his scent. Thrace is fuming and is about to rip strips off anyone who even glances at him. His power to move whatever he likes is not currently working on the wayward Monster, for reasons unknown. He is unable to bring Dainn to him to yell at in person, so he is yelling at everyone else instead. It is in our best interests to find him quickly.

I follow the trail all the way to the back door of Kate's house. I growl, low and angry. He shouldn't be here. I'm unable to knock in my demon dog form, so I glare through the window. I see her kitchen, but not her and not him. He is definitely still here, though. I pad around to the front and staring through the windows, my hot breath steaming up the cold windows, I see them on the couch. He is lying down with his head on Kate's lap, fast asleep, while she has her hand on his head and has her head on the arm of the couch, her eyes closed, but not asleep. Her breathing isn't heavy enough. My sensitive ears can pick up even the slightest sound, so I can hear her soft pant. She isn't afraid, but she isn't relaxed either. She is wary.

Her eyes suddenly pop open and she sees me glaring at her. Her gaze meets mine, but she doesn't move a muscle.

Then she licks her lips and it's all I need to shift and press my hand against the window.

She carefully gets up and lays Dainn's head on a cushion and comes to the window. Opening it, she asks, "What are you doing here?"

"The better question is, what is *he* doing here?"

She looks over her shoulder and sighs. "Can't you see how much pain he is in?"

Blinking quickly, I glance at Dainn.

Pain? From what?

"What do you mean? Is he hurt?" I can't smell any blood.

Kate rolls her pretty eyes. "Mental pain," she says, her sexy lips pursed. "Being here soothes him."

"Is that what he said?" I scoff. I'll give it to him; he pulled a fast one and it worked.

"That is what I know. I can see when a creature is having difficulties. Why can't you?"

I press my lips together, my eyes narrowed. "How are you helping him?"

She shrugs. "I don't know exactly. But he is resting now and I'm not going to disturb him, so go now."

"You're kicking me out?"

"You aren't even in," she points out.

"Humph," I mutter, thoroughly pissed off now. "Thrace is going to have his hide when I tell him he's here."

"Don't tell him, then," she tuts, shaking her head.

"Then Thrace will have *my* hide." I'm not thrilled by that thought.

She giggles. "I doubt the big bad Monster dog is scared."

I can't help but snicker. "Oh, you have no idea." I know she doesn't know about Thrace's real form, and he will go as long as he can without her finding out.

Her lips curve up into a smile and she surprises me by leaning through the window opening to kiss my nose softly.

"You are a very confusing woman," I mutter.

"That's because I'm very confused," she says quietly. "I know what my head thinks, but my heart is all over the place."

"Go with your heart." I cup her face and stare into her eyes, falling for her in ways that I never knew were possible. Despite who she is, her very being is sweet and kind and vulnerable, but she is also so strong.

"Hmm."

She sighs and looks back at the couch.

"Go to him," I whisper. "I will see you tomorrow."

She nods and without another word, closes the window and crosses over to the sleeping Monster on her couch. She tenderly lifts his head up and curls her legs up, settling her head back on the arm. Kate closes her eyes and with a wave of what I know is love wash over me, I turn from her.

Tilting my head when I see the small dog on the garden path, staring at me, I ask, "What do *you* want?"

He sniffs the air but doesn't move.

"I recognize you," I accuse the pup. "I ate your master yesterday, didn't I?"

He whimpers at me and lowers his head to the ground.

"Go away," I growl.

The dog doesn't move.

Huffing, I stalk past it and bend down to shift. My back cracks with bliss as I become the enormous black Monster dog.

I look back over my shoulder and give the small pup an imperious glare, but all it does is make him come forward.

Ignoring him, I cross over the road and walk a little way down the street, when I hear a soft bark behind me.

Turning again, I see the dog has followed me.

Baring my teeth has no effect on him. He is a determined little shit.

Fine.

I let him catch up with me, wagging his tail, his tongue lolling out. I flick my tail at him and curl it around his small, soft furry body and lift him off his feet to place him on my back. He's cute and I always wanted a furry friend. So he's tiny and can't shift into a human, but who cares? He can stay with me and come back to our world with us. I did kill his master after all. He has nowhere else to go and if he hangs around this town much longer, he will be eaten alive just like his master was.

I've got you, little buddy. You're mine now.

Satisfied by my good deed and also feeling all warm inside, I head back to Thrace, not knowing how I'll explain this, but anyone who touches my little pup, will meet their end.

Sixteen

Kate

I wake up, stiff and cold. Also alone. Groaning, I stretch my legs out and look around. It is still fairly early, but Dainn isn't here, and Doris isn't up yet.

Coming fully awake, I gulp. "Uhm," I mutter and rise quickly, rushing into the kitchen to find it empty and then racing to the stairs, flying up them two at a time and bursting into Doris's room.

"Doris!" I yell, coming to a skidding halt when I see her in bed reading. "You're okay." I breathe out in relief.

She peers at me over the top of her reading glasses. "Why wouldn't I be?" she asks.

"Just checking," I state. "I'll pop the kettle on!" I turn and leave her room, closing the door behind me and rushing back down the stairs, glad that Dainn was good on his word not to hurt her...or me, for that matter. I swing by the sitting room, to peer in my bag, but I still can't find a key. When I turn, I smile and pick up the two marigolds that Dainn must've plucked from the back garden and left for me on the couch. He's sweet. I hope being here helped quiet the noise in his head. I know how that is. It is no joke, and I will help any living creature I can who suffers from mental pain.

Ambling into the kitchen, seeing the sun shining in the window, I glance at the clock while I fill the kettle up with water. It's only seven o'clock, but I need to start getting ready to go into the library. Although, as I place the kettle back on the counter and flick the switch, I wonder *why* I have to go to the library. Who is going to come in apart from Doris and the crazy snake Monster? Maybe no one would notice if I took the day off and hung out here with my new bestie.

I grab two mugs from the cupboard and then a movement outside catches my eye. My gaze is drawn to the window where I see a dark-haired woman rush past. That being odd in itself, what with the kitchen overlooking my back garden, I suddenly scream.

"Aahhhhhh!"

The woman outside slumps against the windows. Doris comes running in to see what's going on, just in time to see the outside woman's bloody hands splay out on the pane either side of her head before she slides down the window, leaving a bloody trail.

"Oh, my Jesus," Doris mutters.

Then we both jump a mile as a Monster follows her into the garden, sniffing wildly. His face swims into view in the window and we freeze, clutching onto each other, eyes wide, hearts hammering and palms sweating.

He looks like Thrasher and Dainn, that type of Monster but it isn't either one of them. This Monster's eyes are flashing a vivid red. He plasters his tongue to the window and laps the blood from the glass, as we stand there stock fucking still.

"Is the door locked?" Doris hisses in my ear as we watch the Monster bend down and then hear the crunch of bones.

My armpits are so sweaty right now, I can feel it dripping down my sides.

"I don't know," I murmur back, so quietly, I don't think she heard me.

Our eyes are suddenly riveted to the door handle of the back door. We tighten our grip on each other, and back away slowly as the handle starts to turn.

"Fuck," I whisper in panic. "Fuck."

"Oh, Harold. I'll be seeing you soon..." Doris mutters.

The door creaks open a fraction, and all I can think of suddenly is that I need to oil the hinges.

Not that I'll be alive to do it in a few seconds' time.

"Be ready to run out the front door on the count of three," I whisper. "One, two..."

My mouth drops open in shock when a Monster so enormous and so terrifying, drifts past the window, its tentacles flying around.

"What the hell is that?" Doris asks aghast. "An octopus?"

"Noooo, that would be a Kraken," I hiss, frozen to the spot in terror. I can't move. It's like my feet have turned to lead.

"Oh, Jesus," she mutters again.

The Kraken whips a huge, thick tentacle out and wraps it around the body of the Monster who was trying to get into the house. It lifts the flailing creature high off the ground and then opens its giant maw, dropping the would-be intruder in, kicking and screaming.

"Oh," Doris says, fanning herself. "Oh, my head."

I launch myself forward suddenly and slam the door closed again, turning the key in the lock and backing away again, taking Doris's hand to drag her into the sitting room.

Not that a locked fucking door is going to stop those Monsters from getting inside.

"The key," Doris says. "You need to pull your big girl

panties on, Kate and see that key. Give it to them and send them on their way back to wherever the hell it is they came from. Did you see what it did to Lynda? It *ate* her. It fucking ate her, Kate!"

She is going a bit hysterical, which levels my head. One of us needs to keep our wits about us, so she gets to have her meltdown now and I'll delay mine until later. I snatch up my bag again and kneeling down, I empty the contents onto the coffee table.

"Where is it?" I ask her. "Show it to me."

"Here," she says, gesturing wildly at the entire coffee table.

"Doris, please. I need you to calm down and show me where it is," I reply, trying not to lose it when I see the Kraken gliding past the front windows, but leaving us alone and heading away from the house.

I sit back on my heels and just...stop.

"Thrace," I murmur, knowing it has to be true. He saved me from the snake in the library and now the human-eating fiend outside. "Thrace is the Kraken."

I feel all the blood drain from my face, my head going light. I had sex with that thing. Oh, my fucking fuck. I lower my forehead to the coffee table and try to breathe but there is no air. Someone has sucked it all out of the room and I can't take a breath. My lungs start to burn and the panic sets in. Sitting up, I gasp for air, clutching at my throat.

"It's okay, dear," Doris says, stepping up and coming to my aid.

Our roles have reversed and it's my turn to go into a spin. She rubs my back and says soothing things until I feel the walls that were pressing in on me, move back slightly and my blurry vision clears.

She presses something against my palm, but all I can feel is her skin. "I still can't see it," I pant.

"Try, Kate. No pressure or anything, but really fucking try, okay," she says quietly.

I nod and close my eyes, willing myself to believe in... anything to make this nightmare go away.

Seventeen

Kate

"It's not working," I say with a huff and stand up. Pacing up and down like a caged tiger, I let out a growl and shake my fists at the coffee table where Doris eventually had to put the key, because I can't see it or feel it.

"Maybe you're overthinking it," she says kindly. "Perhaps a cup of tea would help?"

"Maybe," I mutter, but then our gazes lock.

I lick my lips; her face goes rigid.

Neither of us wants to go back into the kitchen with the remains of Lynda laying outside on the garden path.

After a beat, I figure it's my house, my responsibility. "I'll go," I mutter.

"I'll come with you," Doris says bravely.

I grab her hand and squeeze it tightly. "I'm so sorry about your friend."

"It's not your fault, love. This situation is...well, it's

fucking crazy. I just wish I hadn't seen it. Lynda lives at the back of me. We used to chat with a cup of tea while we pegged the washing out. Lived...she *lived* at the back of me."

"Oh, Doris." I pull her into my arms, giving her a big, much-needed hug. For both her and me. She returns it fiercely, but then pulls away and becomes the no-nonsense woman that I've come to adore in such a short space of time.

But then a frown creases my brow. "Wait. She lived at the back of you?"

Doris nods her confirmation.

"Then why did she end up in my back garden?" I ask. "You live a ten-minute walk from here. Why *my* garden, all the way down the other end of town?"

She purses her lips and suddenly becomes the champion of glare avoidance.

"Doris!" I snap. "What do you know?"

"Nothing," she says, but that is the biggest lie I've ever been told, and there's been some doozies after my parents died.

Yes, we'll come over and sit with you while you cry,

Yes, we'd be happy to help you with the funeral.

Of course we'll take care of everything.

Come and stay with us until you feel better.

In the end, they all turned out to be lies. Big, fat, sad lies.

I blink back the tears and fix my stare on Doris.

"Don't lie to me, not after everything," I state, folding my arms over my chest.

"I'm not lying," she says, meeting my heated gaze with one of her own. I tapped into her own sense of morality and now she will spill. "Your parents..." She sighs and rubs her hand over her face. "Let's get that tea."

She walks into the kitchen, and I have no choice but to follow her. Both of us ignoring the bloodstained window like pros, she turns the kettle on again and we wait in silence. The only sound is the bubbling of the water heating up. I want to yell at her to tell me about my parents, what about them? Are they *alive*? But I grip my hands in front of me tightly, waiting until she is ready.

A few minutes later she hands me a big steaming mug and I accept it. I follow her back into the sitting room, and she finally says, "Sit."

I do, just because it will hopefully move this along a little bit. My stomach is about to eat itself with the anxiety that is currently plaguing me.

Doris sits next to me and turns to face me. "Your parents were special, Kate. I didn't know it at first, although I definitely know they weren't from around here."

I frown because as far as I know, they were both born here and lived here until they died.

"They were posh and well educated and as far as I knew had always been here. That is until one day I saw something that I definitely wasn't privy to and in some ways wish I hadn't, but at the same time, oh, it opened up my eyes and my world in ways I couldn't even imagine."

"What do you mean?"

"I'm not supposed to say," she says irritatingly. "Your parents wanted you to find your own destiny."

"*Destiny*?" I splutter. "What is this...a book?"

"Well, kind of." She chews her lip.

I blink slowly. "You're going to have to do way better than that."

"I know, I'm trying to figure out how to say it out loud," she replies.

I wait impatiently as she gathers her thoughts and I daren't even try to think about what she's saying yet until I have all the facts.

"Your parents came from a book," she says eventually, sighing as she must know how ridiculous it sounds. "From a fantasy land with enchanted forests and great big castles, plus creatures from all the spectrum of Monster."

"Erm," I stammer, trying to take that in but failing miserably. "Don't be silly." I scoff and splutter, but she grabs my hand to draw my attention back to her.

"I saw your mom in the back of the library one day, with her hands in a book, literally. She was sucking the words up, under her skin."

"What was she doing," I ask, eyes wide.

"Trying to get home. That's what they told me and that's all I know."

"Was I born here or there?"

"I honestly don't know, Kate. I promise that is all I know. She swore me to secrecy and made me promise that I'd look out for you if anything happened to them."

"And then it did. They died in a car accident...or did they?" I can feel the panic descend again.

"I don't know, Kate," Doris says, shaking her head. "I don't know anything except what I've told you."

I nod slowly, trying to process this. "Do you think they came from the world where the Monsters came from?"

"Possibly. Although, I'm starting to think something else is afoot here."

"What do you mean?"

"Hold that thought."

She stands up and disappears up the stairs, returning shortly with the copy of Hell's Belle.

She opens it, facing outwards and says, "Look."

Blank pages.

"Does that mean the characters from that book are also... here?" I gulp.

She shrugs. "I have a feeling that the creatures from many books are also here."

"Fuck," I mutter, my brain swimming with all of this information. "Well, fucking fuck."

"Hey," a female voice says from behind me, scaring the shit out of me. "That's my line."

Eighteen

Thrasher

"What is going on with all of this shit?" I bellow over the noise. A Monster that looks a bit like a Behemoth, but on a much smaller scale, is howling and making a racket as Eerie battles with it down the road from Kate's.

"The only thing I can imagine that makes sense is that Kate seems to have control over all the books in the library and these have also come to life and are trying to claim her," Thrace informs me in the way that is super annoying and imperious.

Eerie's annoying little pet is yapping furiously, but shuts the fuck up when I growl at it. He doesn't back down though. He's got spunk. I supposed I could learn to tolerate the furball.

"Well, that's quite detailed, you asshole," I snarl. "How long have you been sitting on that?"

He doesn't get to reply as a beast twice my size launches into me from out of nowhere, knocking me off my feet. It lands on top of me and bares sharp venomous teeth before it leans down and tries to take a chunk out of my neck.

"Fuck you!" I yell, bringing my knee up to its nuts area. Whether it has any or not, who knows, but it backs off slightly, enough for me to ball my fist up and punch it in the face, hard enough to knock it back.

I turn to Thrace for a bit of help, but he is occupied by another Serpent that is hissing and snarling like a fiend.

"Fuck's sake," I mutter and haul my battered body to my feet and face off with the creature that kind of looks like me but is way uglier. "You want a piece of me?" I growl, fists up.

I don't think this beast can speak. It howls a response and, head down, slams into me, but this time I'm ready. I punch it in the head before I turn the table and clamp my teeth down on its neck. I pull back and rip through its flesh, killing it.

"I've had enough!" I shout at the sky, hoisting the beast over my head and throwing it as far as I can.

It thunks to the ground a little way from my feet.

Thrace snorts with amusement, having dealt with this Serpent.

"What? It's twice my size," I point out. "I'm surprised I managed to pick it up at all."

Might as well boast about the things you did rather than be embarrassed about things you failed at.

I hear Dainn, snarling and hissing nearby and turn to face him, pissed off that he disappeared on us last night. I watch him take out a small beastie by eating it with two bites and then I march up to him and demand an explanation.

"Where were you?"

"Leave him alone," Eerie says, having shifted to his human form so he could, presumably, pick up his furball.

Dainn's gaze goes to his and they share a knowing look that excludes Thrace and more importantly, *me*.

"Dainn?" I ask, stepping closer to him and cutting off his line of sight to Eerie.

"I was with Kate," he mumbles.

"Oh?" I ask, folding my arms over my chest. "All night?"

Thrace comes closer, fury emanating from every pore. "Kate's?" he snarls. "You were warned to stay away from her."

Dainn looks down, but once again, Eerie steps up to defend him. "Look, just leave it. He needed to be close to her. We all do. So what? We are still no closer to finding this fucking key, so it's not like it would have helped having him searching anyway, seeing as we're distracted with all these other fuckers."

I narrow my eyes and look between the two of them. "What is going on here?" I ask, pointing first at Dainn and then at Eerie. "Since when did you two become such great buddies?"

"Since Kate made me realize that we all need her in different ways," Eerie says, facing off with me. He looks like he is about to burst into his demon dog form when another round of fight the Monster begins and he doesn't have time before some poor slimy fucker tries to eat his pet.

Even I give him a look of distaste when he grabs the slimy thing and rips it in half with his bare hands. Green goo sprays all over him and up his face, in his mouth, but he's gone feral on the slime beast and well, that's that.

"So does this mean we all get time on our own with her?" I ask a damn good question.

"If she wants you to be near her," Eerie chokes out, spitting goo all over the road.

"No," Thrace states. "This is against all the rules. Our mission was supposed to be that once she pulled us out of our world, we convinced her to come back with us where she belongs. Our asses are on the line here and this madness is slowing us down. Losing the key was an unfortunate event, but it has to be here somewhere. All of these extra fuckers need to be taken down. I will not have anything stand in the way of us bringing Kate home. We have been distracted by our cocks and our..." He waves his hand at Eerie's furball, "...whatever the fuck this is, when we need to be focused on the key."

"You're telling us shit we already know," I grumble.

"Then why are you still standing here?" he roars, losing his temper in a way that sends his tentacles flying off in all directions. I duck, but Dainn is too slow and gets whacked around the head by one.

"Oww," he groans, rubbing his skull.

"Fuck's sake," I mutter. "Fine. Cocks, Monsters and furballs be damned. We are finding this fucking key today if it kills us. Because let's face it, if we don't find it and take the Mistress of the Book home soon, we are dead anyway."

"Precisely," Thrace mutters.

With that doom and gloom cloud over our heads, we scatter, and I dive under a bush, scrabbling around in the dirt until I've dug up the whole thing and decided the key is not here and I move onto the next.

Nineteen

Kate

Turning slowly, I have no idea what to expect. Taking in the unbelievably attractive redhead with boobs to die for, which are encased in a tiny leather top to match her tight black leather pants, I fix my gaze on her green eyes.

"Who are you?" I ask tentatively.

"The Devil," Doris whispers in my ear. "Annabelle, right?" she adds louder to the woman.

"Yep," she says, pressing her full red lips together. "And you are?"

"Doris," she says. "This is Kate."

I glare at her. What is she doing?

"What?" Doris asks with a shrug. "She's reasonable and she can speak."

"*She* wants to know what the fucking fuck, *if you don't mind*, is going on here," Annabelle says, and then looks over her shoulder. "Oh, I wondered if you'd also come."

We follow her gaze and then take a step back from the

giant *man* that enters the sitting room from the kitchen ducking his head low to avoid hitting it on the lintel.

"Whoa, mama," Doris murmurs, fanning herself with her hand. "War. It's fucking War."

"What?" I stammer, taking in the white eyes of this so-called War.

"Eyes over here, if you don't mind," Annabelle clips out, snapping her fingers at us.

"Erm," I mutter as Doris decides to play with fire and moves forward to stand next to him. She gazes adoringly up at him, stroking his arm lovingly.

"Oh, for the love of all things, unholy," Annabelle says. "Can't take you anywhere."

He grunts his response, but seemingly indulges Doris with a dazzling smile.

The old woman practically faints on the spot.

"Jesus," I mutter, but then slam my lips shut as Annabelle gives me a filthy glare. "Sorry," I add like a fool. I mean, come on. The Devil? What the fuck is this...?

Oh, yeah. I keep forgetting...a book. Or many books. Come to life in my fucking house.

"Err, Mr. War, do you think you could do me a favor?" Doris asks.

"Depends," he says.

"There's a...woman in the back garden. Can you do something with her?"

"Doris!" I exclaim.

"What do you mean 'woman'?" Annabelle asks, eyes narrowed.

Without waiting for an answer, she stalks into the kitchen and yanks open the back door. We follow her, because, like, why wouldn't we?

Annabelle says, "Oh, her, you mean?"

I nod slowly.

Doris averts her gaze.

"What exactly do you want him to do with her? She's dead and half eaten by the looks of it."

"Dispose of her," Doris mutters. "She is just lying there waiting for another Monster to come and finish her off. Can you, I dunno, do something?"

Annabelle shrugs and leaves it to War to run his hand over the dead body of Lynda and she dissipates to ash. "Now. Why are we here and how do we get back home?"

"Good question. We know you came out of the book, but we don't know how, or why, or how to get you home," I say, and give her a grimace because I know how lame that sounds.

"Great," she mutters. "I take it we aren't the only ones."

I shake my head. Doris has clammed up, partly out of respect for poor, departed Lynda and probably also because she is still mooning over this War guy.

"Is it true you have a thirteen-inch cock?" she suddenly blurts out.

"WHAT?" I choke on my saliva at her intrusive question.

Annabelle snickers uncontrollably. "Why don't you show her, dear?" she snorts in between bouts of laughter.

"Fuck off," War replies, disgruntled.

"Gives a whole new meaning to a horse's dick!" Doris squeals, her laughter coming thick and fast now.

That's when the penny drops. War is the *Horseman* of War.

Jesus fucking Christ. Can this day get any weirder?

"Well, on that note, I'm going out there to see what's going on," Annabelle says.

"Wait," I say. "You don't seem like Monsters. Why did you come out of the book?"

She glances around, her lips pursed, almost as if she is debating whether to tell us something. "Well, we were with another at the time. He is *definitely* construed as a Monster. He must be out there somewhere. We need to find him."

"Wh-what does he look like?" I stammer, hoping it's not the Monster that Thrace ate. This Devil seems reasonable *now,* but if a Kraken ate her lover, then I think reason will go out of the window.

"A Hellhound!" Doris exclaims. "Am I right? Is Elijah here?"

Annabelle rolls her eyes at me. "Calm her down, would you? I need to find my puppy."

I nod dumbly and watch as they leave the house, engulfed in flames.

Sitting down heavily on the couch, I splutter. "This is... this is...beyond..."

"I know!" Doris says. "Isn't it exciting!"

"That's not what I was going to say." I give her a glare and she quietens down. "Poor Lynda."

"At least she won't be devoured by a scavenger."

I meet her stare and I see the sorrow. She is just trying to make the best of this awful, frightening situation. "Yeah."

"Okay, we need a plan. Do you think you can show me which book my parents were...from?" It sounds weird coming from my lips.

She nods. "I think so, but that means..."

We both glance at the front door. "Going to the library," I finish for her.

"Yep."

A few seconds pass and I clear my throat. "Tell me where it is, and I'll go and bring it back here."

"No, if you step out that door, then I'm going too."

"Stop being stubborn!" I yell at her.

"Same to you!"

"Fine!" I yell. "Let's freshen up and then we'll both go out there and walk the ten minutes to the library."

"Fine!" she yells back.

"I'll go shower first," I inform her, my devious plan in motion.

"Oh, the fuck you will!" she roars. "You are not going to ditch me while I'm brushing my teeth."

"How are you going to stop me?" I ask, triumphantly folding my arms over my chest.

"Like this," she says primly and picks up her mug of cold tea from the coffee table and dumps the contents over my head, drowning me in tannin and milk as she heads for the stairs with more speed than I would've given her credit for, leaving me spluttering and cursing her ingenuity.

Twenty

Kate

After waiting impatiently for Doris to finish her shower in *my* en-suite – the other bathroom only has a bath, and you cannot run the hot tap while the shower is on. She knew this because I told her on the way home yesterday. Crafty witch.

She gives me a smug smile as she disappears into her room while I'm toweling the tea out of my hair. I strip off quickly and jump in the shower, washing up at super speed and diving back out. I'm nervous and anxious and the anxiety is driving me to get a move on. Once I have the book, and we can come back home, actually *make* it back home, I'll feel better and then can decide what I plan on doing with it. As it stands, I have no idea, I just know in my soul that I *need* that book.

Doris is waiting for me when I head down the stairs in sweats and running shoes, just in case we have to run. Which in all likelihood, is a given. Doris is similarly dressed, her bright pink leg warmers and headband in place to complete the look of an elderly woman going for a power walk. I smile and forgive her. She has guts of iron and if it wasn't for her, I'd be a mess right now.

"Ready?"

She nods briskly.

We both stare at the door. All seems quiet on the outside.

I step forward and stick my finger at the edge of the small curtain next to the door and push it to the side. Peering out, I can't see any Monsters or people running for their lives.

"I think it's clear," I murmur.

"Let's go then," she says. "Here."

I turn back to her to see what she's trying to hand me.

Blinking once, I bite my lip, trying not to laugh.

"What? The other ones are still in the dishwasher from last night. *Someone* forgot to switch it on before they went to bed."

I recall that *someone* was me and I'd gotten distracted by Dainn coming over.

With a smile, I take the small, serrated knife from her and grip it tightly. She has another one in her left hand and pulls a big meat fork out of her bag to brandish in her right.

Reaching out with a shaky hand, I slide the bolt back carefully and wince when it makes a small squeak that I have never noticed before, but I swear it has never done prior to this moment. Once that is all the way back, I turn the key and jump when Doris says, "Wait."

She rushes over to the coffee table and picks up my bag along with the copy of Hell's Belle. She shoves it inside and then hands me my bag.

"Thanks," I mutter. I was so caught up in my anxiety, that I'd forgotten all about the supposed key in my bag. I sling it over my shoulder and then turn the handle slowly, stepping forward to peek out, scanning the street for nefarious creatures before I open it wide enough for us to slip out. Closing it quickly once we are on the garden path, I lock it and place the key in the pocket of my hoodie, so it's easily accessible.

And so, armed with a couple of steak knives and a meat fork, we two brave soldiers head off down the street, eyes peeled for Monsters and the Zombie Apocalypse alike, on a mission to find the book that may give us some answers to this crazy, crazy affair.

* * *

Ten fairly uneventful minutes later, we see the library swim into view and we both breathe out in relief. I say *fairly* uneventful because while we didn't come across any Monsters, we did hear screams and growls in the distance, which almost made me pee myself and made us pick up the pace somewhat.

Breathless and flushed, I reach into my pocket for the key to unlock the library and we slip inside. I lock it behind us and replace the key in my pocket. Casting nervous glances at each other, we head into the dim building, but all seems quiet.

"Where is it?" I whisper.

"Right at the back," she replies.

With a nod, I scamper forward, Doris hot on my heels, to the back stacks. Frowning, I turn to her. "Are you sure? This is the medical non-fiction section."

"Quite sure. That's it there." She points to a blank space at the very end of the shelf below the top one.

I growl with frustration. "I can't fucking see it!" I exclaim louder than I'd intended.

Doris scowls at me. "This is becoming a problem, Kate," she says in a no-nonsense voice that definitely feels mom-ish in its tone.

"Sorryyyyy," I whine, reverting to a pain-in-the-ass teen when confronted with epic failure.

"It's fine," Doris says, getting over her annoyance, but then she peers at me. "You've worked here all this time and you never *once* wondered why there was blank space there?"

"I never noticed it before," I reply with a shrug.

"How is that even possible?" she mutters under her breath.

"Oh, I don't know, Doris," I snap, getting pissed off. "How is *any* of this possible?"

"Good point," she says with a sheepish look. "I take it you can't feel it, either?"

I poke the blank space but feel only air. "Nope."

"Hold your bag out under it," Doris instructs.

I do as commanded, opening my bag and hoisting it up.

She reaches out with her steak knife and gingerly tips the book – I presume, obviously – into the bag. "Don't want to touch it," she mutters.

"Don't blame you."

She gives me a grateful smile and then she asks, "Can you feel the weight of it in your bag?"

I shake my head, then we turn our heads sharply as we hear voices behind us, pissed off and bordering on frightening.

Twenty-One

Kate

"This is getting increasingly frustrating!" Thrace's voice echoes around the quiet library.

We hear things scattering.

I motion to Doris to move closer to me. We inch forward and closer to the stacks so we can peek around and see what's going on.

Thrace and Eerie are there, both looking as livid as snakes.

"What makes these assholes think they can take *our* Queen?" Thrace bellows.

Queen?

"One of them said she is the Book Goddess," Eerie snarls.

I cast a sidelong glance at Doris, who is staring at me with her eyebrow raised. I shrug. It's the first I've heard of this. And we don't know they're talking about me. Maybe some other Book Goddess is walking around that we aren't aware of. Annabelle, maybe. She was pretty Goddess-like. Okay, the opposite, but still. More so than me.

"Enrico and Josefina are going to skin us alive if we don't bring her back soon," Thrace continues, earning himself an exasperated look from Eerie.

In the next second, the names bounce around my head.

Enrico and Josefina. Enrico and Josefina. Enrico and Josefina. Henry and Jo. Henry and Jo. Henry and Jo?

"Henry and Jo," I mutter out loud and then flinch when Doris squeezes my hand hard, and Thrace stops his tirade about being skinned alive to glare at the stacks.

"Kate?" he snaps.

I clamp my lips shut.

I squeak as a tentacle whips around the stacks and encircles both me and Doris and drags us out from behind the protection of the books.

"You eavesdrop now?" he asks sardonically, tightening his hold on us a fraction.

"We were here first," Doris chimes in. "So if anyone is intruding, it's you two." She points her finger between the two, even though her arm is pinned to her side. Her gaze wanders over to Eerie's extensive manhood on show and she sighs.

I shudder with grossness.

"You have a smart mouth on you for someone bound up," Thrace informs her, but without menace.

"I speak my mind. Why be all shy and reserved?" she says with a sniff.

Thrace's gaze lands on me. "Yes, I quite agree. Dear Kate, what are your thoughts on this?"

"Hmm," I murmur, my cheeks heating up.

After a few moments, he releases his hold on us. "You shouldn't be out here. It's dangerous right now."

"We know. Poor Lynda," Doris murmurs.

"We needed something," I say and then wish I'd kept my mouth shut.

"Oh?" Thrace asks as Eerie's ears perk up...along with the dog's parked next to him that I've only just noticed.

"Books!" Doris exclaims too loudly. "If we are to be holed up, we need entertainment."

"Yep," I agree, thankful she is quicker on her feet than me.

"So, you risked your lives to come here for some books," he states, not believing a word of it. And why should he. It's a lie. Sort of. We do need *a* book. One specific book that I can't even see.

"Indeed," he murmurs. "You should go home."

"On our way," Doris says.

"Allow me," Thrace says and snaps his fingers. In a puff of smoke, we land back in my sitting room, startled and a bit nauseous.

"Eurgh," Doris moans and dumps her bag on the table with the cutlery jangling inside.

I've still got my knife clutched in my fist, my bag in the other and I dump both of them on the coffee table.

"Do you think he was talking about my parents?" I ask suddenly.

Doris sighs. "It's a bit of a stretch."

"But what if it's not. What if they are still alive and in this book?"

Our conversation is interrupted by a loud knock on the door.

I gesture for Doris to answer it as she does the same to me.

In the end, the impatient knocking drives me forward and picking up the knife again to grip tighter, I open the door. I mean, a flesh-eating Monster isn't going to knock, is it?

Confronted with the sight of Annabelle and War, my gaze then goes to the ginormous creature standing behind them. A dog with three heads and I don't even want to know how many teeth. It's twice the size of Eerie in his demon dog form, and I think just a tiny amount of pee comes out when he bares those sharp teeth at me.

I hastily find Annabelle's gaze again and give her a shaky smile.

"Where's my book?" she asks, tapping her foot impatiently.

"In my bag..." I start, but Doris is one step ahead and thrusts it at me.

Switching knife for book, I take it and hold it out to Annabelle.

She gives me a scathing glare. "No, dearie. You have to do whatever it is you do and send us home. The longer I'm gone, the worse things are going to get for me. So, chop-chop." She waves her hand in my direction.

"Err," I stammer and glance at Doris for advice.

"Don't look at me," she mutters.

"Okay, well, here's the thing...I don't..." The Hellhound growls and snaps its three jaws, so I wing it and open the book, facing outwards towards them. I scrunch my eyes up, willing them back into the pages.

Gripping the book tightly and shaking it as I use my will, I crack an eye open to see them still standing in front of me.

"Yeah, can't do it," I state the fucking obvious.

"Look, word on the street is you are some kind of Book Goddess." Her scathing gaze rakes over me, and I squirm uncomfortably. "So, use that magick to send us home."

"I want to. I really do, but I have no idea. This is all new to me. Like today new. I need some help. Got any advice to offer instead of just criticizing?" I snap, losing my nervousness and getting pissed off.

The War man snorts and gives me an amused expression. "The last person to talk to her like that lost his head to a baseball bat," he informs me readily.

"Well, how unfortunate for him. You need *my* help so hands off my head, or you'll be here forever."

"We will be anyway at this rate," Annabelle mutters under her breath. "Here's the deal. Send us home and I won't get Killian to hold you down while Elijah eats you. How's that?"

I assume Killian is War and yeah, nope. He could pin me down with his pinky.

"We need her alive," Killian tuts at her. "She is right about that."

"Thank you," I huff and hold the book up again. "Less pressure, less stress and I'm sure I can do this." Mm-hm, big, fat lie.

I close my eyes and inhale deeply, forgetting about all other thoughts except Enrico and Josefina and after a few seconds, I hear Doris gasp.

"You did it, Kate. You did it."

"What?" I ask, my eyes flying open. "Are you serious?"

"Look at the pages, dear girl." She takes the book from me and turns it around.

The pages are filled with words and my eyes fill with tears.

"I did it."

Twenty-Two

Thrace

Glaring at Eerie, I know he is hiding something. "I'm surprised you didn't smell her in here," I say, doing some digging.

He shrugs. "I knew."

"Then why didn't you say?"

He huffs out a breath. "I am sick of this to and fro. I wanted to make sure she heard what we were saying so that she would know who she is, and then we could go the fuck home. I hate this place and all these other Monsters trying to claim her, is pissing me off."

I knew it.

"She is far more special than even we thought," I muse. "But it doesn't change anything. Enrico and Josefina sent us on this mission, knowing their daughter was turning thirty human years of age and would unlock the door to our world. But without that key, we are all stuck here."

"And this is all stuff I wanted her to know," Eerie mutters. "In fact, I'm going over there to tell her."

"You can't. She has to decide to come on her own."

"Why? Why can't we just tell her and get this over with?"

"If she doesn't believe it within herself, we won't be going anywhere." I let out a sigh and rub my hand over my face. I'm tired. I'm tired of fighting. I'm tired of being the responsible one. I'm tired of being here without Kate.

"I know you agree with me," Eerie says slyly when he sees how weary I am.

"On a level, yes, I do. I want nothing more than to tell her that she is our Queen and that her parents need her to come home. Without her there, our world is crumbling. Enrico and Josefina are trapped, unable to bring her to them, so it is up to us."

"Then there is only one thing for it," he declares. "We are going to have to convince her, and quickly. I propose each of us spends time with her on her own. Get her on our side, let her know us. Whatever happens during that time, happens. I am *done* fucking about."

I couldn't agree more. "Fine," I say after a beat where I pretended to think about it but didn't have to. "I will go to her now. Somehow convince her to leave her friend and spend time with me, just the two of us. You can go next. Find the boys and tell them of the plan. We each get twelve hours of this world with her and by the end of the two days, if she hasn't decided to believe, then we tell her, and the consequences be damned."

He smiles, a slow sexy smile that I've missed. Since we came here, our time together has been at loggerheads, with only minimal close contact due to the stress and frustration of this situation.

"I love it when you get all leader on our asses," he murmurs.

I raise an eyebrow. "Do you, now? And here I thought it pissed you off."

"Sometimes," he admits. "Not now."

"Come over here and show me then."

The invitation does not need to be repeated. He takes a step forward and cups the back of my neck, kissing me deeply, bruising our lips with his urgency.

"She was turned on when she watched us," he murmurs against my lips.

"She was," I agree.

He bites his bottom lip. "This doesn't mean that I don't want her any less."

Giving him a curious look, I ask, "You are redefining our relationship? Now?"

"Sort of," he says. "I just want it on the record. She is my main priority."

"As she is mine." Now, I'm getting pissed off again. He is acting like I'm trying to convince him otherwise.

"Don't get annoyed. I'm just saying."

"Hmm."

He spins me around suddenly and presses himself against my back, his arms going around me, his mouth on the side of my neck. I grab his hand and move it slowly down to my hardening cock. He squeezes and I let him go to undo my pants. He reaches in and pulls my cock out, fisting it gently, a low moan escaping his lips.

"I've missed this."

"Me too," I murmur, dropping my head back enough for him to kiss me again.

His tongue works against mine, arousing me further. I'm rock-hard within seconds. He knows what to do next. He turns me, dropping to his knees and takes me in his mouth, grazing his teeth down my length before he circles his tongue around the shaft and sucks roughly all the way up to the top.

"Fuck," I groan, fisting my hand in his dark hair. I can feel myself relaxing and inhaling deeply, I add, "Stand up."

He does as I ask, and I position him over one of the display tables at the back of the library. I am seeping pre cum, which I use to lube up my fingers with a bit of saliva to ease my way. My fingers slide over his asshole before I thrust one inside, making him rasp.

"Yes, Thrace," he groans. "More."

I add another finger, stretching him gently before I think he's ready for me. I withdraw and grab my cock, positioning it at the hole. I slowly guide my cock into him, taking hold of his hips as I bury myself as deep into him as I can go. I stop moving to give him time to get used to my invasion.

"Take your cock in your hand," I murmur.

He does and starts to jerk off gently.

That's when I pull back before I slam my hips against him, roughly, quickly, riding his ass while he fists his cock to help make himself come.

"That's it," I pant, feeling the climax building slowly. "How does that feel?"

"So good," he rasps. "I'm going to come."

He grunts and stiffens up before he shoots his load all over his palm.

"Fuck, yes. Fuck, yes," I pant, harder and harder.

I thrust faster and harsher and then I groan, dark and low as I spurt my cum into his ass, gripping his hips tightly, shoving my cock even deeper into him, causing him to moan in pleasure.

My breath coming quickly, I pull out of him and do up my pants. I lean down to kiss the top of his head. "See you in twelve hours."

I puff out in a stream of smoke and land in the house that we have been staying at while we are camped out in this world.

Smiling and feeling more relaxed than I have since I got here, I take a shower, relishing in the cold water hitting my skin and turning my hands to their natural state. Grabbing the soap with one of my appendages, I clean up, looking forward to my time with Kate.

Twenty-Three

Kate

"You know what you have to do now?" Doris asks.

"Try and get the Monsters back into the books?" I reply tentatively. I'm pretty sure that's what she means, but who knows with her.

"Yep. Which means..."

We both glance at the door.

"We need to go back to the library," I say with a sigh.

"Yep again. Wait here."

She disappears into the kitchen, and I hear the dishwasher being opened. I smile when she returns with some bigger kitchen knives than last time, and I hold my hand out for one. She slaps the handle against my palm, turns to pick up my bag and gives me that as well.

"Just one quick check?"

I nod and open my bag, peering inside. "Nope. No parent book, nor a key. *Yet*. I'll get there, Doris. I promise you."

"Don't do it for me, girl. You need to do this for you and you alone."

I give her a grateful smile and then face the front door.

"Wait!" she says and tuts. She goes across to the side table and picks up the pen and pad that I leave there for my shopping lists. "We need a list."

Raising my eyebrow. "You want food?"

"Noo," she says as if I'm a bit dim. "A list of books. Which Monster Romance books have you read lately?"

My cheeks heat up. I don't want to say.

Doris rolls her eyes. "Oh, Kate. I don't care if you read Monster Romance books. Hell, *I* read them. I really don't care if you hide them in crochet magazines or read them on the bus. No one does."

Still, I hesitate. My embarrassment at being caught reading Monster porn, deepening my blush until I feel like my whole head is going to set on fire. "What makes you think it has anything to do with the books I've read?" I croak. "I didn't read Hell's Belle."

"No, but I read it in your house, with you here. I am convinced that you are opening these worlds, Kate, and if that upsets you, I'm sorry but you need to get over it. I'm not blaming you; I'm just trying to help fix this mess. Okay? So, we need a list."

Gulping, I nod. She's right. "There aren't that many. I don't usually bring them home and only read them in the library when I get a few minutes. It takes me ages to finish one."

She nods. "Okay, then we definitely need to head to the library. You ready? You can think about the list on the way."

Relieved that I've been let off the book hook for now, I nod back. "Okay."

We face the door, grim determination on our faces and our knives at the ready when a loud knock makes us both squeal, the fear coursing through me so badly, I nearly vomit. I stumble back, gripping the knife tighter.

"Kate?" A familiar voice calls out and I feel both relieved and scared at the same time.

"Thrace?" I call back.

"Yes, it is me."

Casting a glance at Doris briefly, I stare back at the door. "How do I know?"

"Uhm..."

We hear footsteps leading away in a suspicious manner and then a knock on the sitting room window.

Shifting my gaze, I see Thrace standing there waving.

"It's me. See?"

"But how do I know? You could be some kind of...some kind of..." I struggle for the word.

"Shifter!" Doris calls out. "You could have his face, but not be him. Prove who you are."

We see him sigh and think about Doris's demand. Then he gets a sly look on his face and my head nearly combusts because I know precisely what is going to come out of his mouth.

"Kate, I know you like it when I..."

"It's fine, come in! Come in!" I yell too loudly, launching myself at the door and slamming the bolt back before I yank the door open.

Doris is trying her hardest not to snicker, but the jig is up. She knows and I find that I actually don't care. So what? I had sex with a Monster. Four Monsters. With a total of six cocks between them and some tentacles thrown in. Who the fuck cares?

"Hi," I say breathlessly as he presses past me to get inside. He is close, very close and he smells deliciously of soap and the sea.

"Hi," he replies. "Can we talk?"

"Not right now," Doris interrupts. "You, Mr. Kraken man, need to get us back to the library right now."

Thrace blinks once and then clears his throat. "Mr. Who-now?"

"You heard me." Her hand is on her hip and her gaze is steely. I wouldn't mess with her now if you paid me.

"I see," Thrace mutters. "You are aware..."

"That you are a giant octopus thing, yeah, we know," she says, brushing it off.

My lips are pressed so tightly together so I don't laugh, I'm practically bruising them.

"Indeed." His sharp blue-eyed glare lands on me. "You find this amusing?"

"Not at all," I squeak, but then the flood of laughter erupts, and I snort in his face, much to my own mortification and his entertainment.

"You are not afraid?"

I shake my head, knowing that I'm not. He has done absolutely nothing to make me afraid of him. Okay, well, except threaten me at the beginning, but I know now that was all bluster. He wouldn't hurt me. He needs me. They all do. I know it's more than that. They *want* me. As astounding as that fact is, I know it's true. I felt it during our sex. You can't fake that kind of connection.

"Good," he murmurs. "That's good. Kate. I want to spend some time with you. Alone," he adds, giving Doris a pointed look.

"Library first and then you can do the horizontal mambo later, or vertical, or upside down, however you like it. Kate has work to do to clean up this Monster mess and with a bit of luck, you can all be sent home anon. So, chop-chop." She claps her hands.

"You want me to take you to the library?" he murmurs.

I nod. "If you don't mind? We could walk, but, you know, the danger..."

"Yes, it's very dangerous out there. Very well. I shall do as you request, but I get what I want in return."

"Doris isn't leaving this house." I make that very clear.

"She can stay. *We* will leave," he replies, and snaps his fingers, smoking us to the library where I suddenly discover that performance anxiety is crippling. I'm punched in the gut by the fear of failure, and it brings tears to my eyes.

"You can do this," Doris says kindly, gripping my arm to stop me from collapsing.

"Do what, exactly?" Thrace asks, taking my other arm.

"Send all these Monsters back into the books," I rasp. "We just need to find them."

The look of astonishment on his face is enough to relax me slightly.

"You can do this?"

I nod with a small smile. "Yes, I think I can."

"Go, Kate, go!" Doris cheers from the sidelines and I pull my big girl panties up.

This town is depending on me, and I will not let them down any more than I already have by bringing them all here. How I did that can be solved another time. Right now, it's clean up in aisle Monster and I intend to do this without further complaint.

I pull away from Doris and Thrace, and march over to the Paranormal Romance stacks with determination. Grabbing the nearest book, I flick through it and finding it blank, I turn back to them. "I haven't read this one, but look..." I show them the pages. "We are going to have to do this the hard way."

"What's that?" Thrace asks, curiously.

I give the front doors of the library a disgusted glare. "I'm going to have to go out there, find some Monsters and see if they will go back into this book. If they don't, move on and try again."

"Oh, that doesn't sound good,' Doris chimes in. "There has to be an easier way?" She taps her chin. "Oh, I know!" she exclaims suddenly. "Look online at the reviews. There's always someone who gives an irritating, long-winded synopsis of the book, blow-by-blow. We can find out from them. Who knew they'd have their uses?"

"Not me," I mutter, but knowing she is right. It's better than my idea anyway. "Get to it then." I wave my hand at her and she pulls her phone out of her bag and gets to work, as I do the same on the next blank book.

Thrace watches us compile a decent list and an hour later, we have three books, with eight sets of Monsters to hunt down and send home.

It's a start.

Twenty-Four

Kate

The three of us make our way out of the library and down the street on the hunt for the Monsters on our list. Turns out, with Thrace's input, we have less to hunt down and return. He estimates that they have already killed about a dozen or so. I guess their stories just...faded? Who knows? I'm sorry to say that I don't.

After about an hour of searching with no luck, I huff out a breath of frustration. "This is pointless! There's no Monsters here."

"Oh, they're here," Thrace replies.

"You need to leave," Doris announces.

"Excuse me?" he replies.

"No, she's right," I chime in. "You are putting them off from approaching."

"How? As far as they know, I'm just a human walking along with two other humans."

"Yeah, not so much. You don't even come across as a man.

You are a Monster, any other Monster can see that," I say, knowing I'm right. He's too 'something' to be a regular old human. I can't put my finger on it, but he's different and I don't just mean his tentacles, which are currently disguised as fingers.

"Then what would you like me to do?" he asks, perplexed. "I can't stop being what I am."

"Noo, but you can take a step back and let us do what we need to do," I reply, shooing him away.

"It's too dangerous, and you are too precious."

Doris sighs. "We get it. You want to keep her safe. But isn't it better to do that by sending the Monsters back into the books?"

Thrace thinks about that for a moment. "I suppose...I will give you one hour and then I will find you."

"Great," I say, relieved he accepted that so easily.

He nods and with narrowed eyes turns to stalk off down the road.

"You aren't buying that, are you?" Doris asks.

"What do you mean?"

"He's going to be right behind us 'keeping you safe'." She uses air quotes which makes me laugh.

"As long as he stays out of the way so we can get this done."

I swallow and turn back the way we were headed and away from Thrace. Not a minute later a huge Behemoth lumbers into view, snarling and growling, flashing its huge claws at us.

I stifle my need to scream and run like a girl and inhale deeply. "Which book?" I ask Doris.

She consults her list rapidly.

"This one," she says, handing me a blank book with a cover that has so much going and is so colorful, it hurts my eyes. I open it, clutching both ends and hold it up so the pages are facing outwards.

"Come on, Kate. Come on," I mutter, closing my eyes, mostly to concentrate, but also so that I can't see it eat me alive if I fail.

Suddenly, I can feel a buzz vibrate through the book and out towards my hands. I open my eyes to see a golden glow light up the shadow from the enormous beast.

"Come on, you fucker," I mutter as it plods closer and closer.

"Kate," Doris mutters urgently. "Do it."

"I'm trying," I grit out.

I can feel its hot breath on my face, its claws are practically scraping my hands clutching the book.

I scrunch my eyes closed again as it roars in my face, and then...

"Is it gone?" I ask.

"Yep," Doris says breezily, as if she wasn't crapping her pants a few moments ago along with me.

I slam the book shut and keep a tight grip on it. "One down..."

"Seven to go."

With grim determination, we head off again. This time my confidence is higher, and I know that it wasn't a fluke. Hopefully, the more I do this, the easier it will become.

No such luck.

As soon as we round a corner and spot the park, we stop.

"Shit."

"Mm-hm."

There are three Monsters crowded together and as soon as they spot us, they turn towards us as one.

I gulp. "Get behind me."

"They're from different books!" Doris is waving her list in my direction.

"Then give me the other one," I say calmly.

"Jesus. Oh, Jesus..." Doris slaps another book into my

hand, and I exhale slowly, pursing my lips and trying to calm my racing heart. If I can do this, we are half-way. I *have* to do this.

"Kate," Thrace's warning voice hisses behind me.

"Go. Away," I snap, holding the books up as the Monsters stop at the sight of Thrace behind me.

"Not a chance," he replies.

"Grrrr," I snarl, but ignore him and, this time keeping my eyes wide open, I grip the books, one in each hand, and hold them up higher.

The Monsters start running away from us, and I turn to Thrace. "Leave now! You aren't helping!"

"I will not leave you to be eaten alive!" he yells back.

"They're getting away!" Doris shouts.

"Dammit! Thrace!"

It takes him a few seconds to capitulate, but he does. "Fine. But you had better not get killed, or I will...I will... grrrrr." He slinks off into the shadows, pissed off but staying out of the way. As soon as the Monsters realize that he isn't protecting us anymore, they turn back and run towards us.

I don't bother telling Doris to leave. She won't, so I just accept that she isn't going anywhere and hold the books up again.

My hands start to shake as the vibrations increase until I can barely hold onto the books anymore.

"Kate."

"Shh."

I feel wetness under my nose and wipe it on my shoulder.

"Kate, stop."

"No," I rasp and taste blood in my mouth. It is pouring out of my nose as I hold onto the books.

"Kate," Doris says, putting her hand over mine.

The flash of light that shoots out of the books and sweeps

the Monsters up, taking them back to their own worlds, astounds the both of us.

I stare at her, as she does me. "What the fuck?"

"What the fuck, indeed," she mutters.

Twenty-Five

Kate

"What was that?" I ask.

"I don't know," she replies.

"What did you...?"

"I don't know."

"Did you know?"

"No."

"Are you some kind of...?"

"I *don't know*!"

Silence.

"Kate! Kate!"

Thrace's voice draws my attention away from Doris and the weird situation we currently find ourselves in.

Wiping my bloody nose grossly on my sleeve, I turn my head towards his voice and then stumble back. "Oh, hell."

We are being stampeded by about a dozen Monsters. "Where the fuck did they come from?" I shriek as Thrace launches himself in front of us to form a Kraken wall that is quite effective.

I'm trembling in fear, paralyzed otherwise. Doris is as still as a statue.

"We need to go," she says eventually.

"No, we need to figure out which of these books they came from."

I hold up the two still in my hands. Doris clutches my wrist, but nothing happens. I shriek as Thrace deals with a couple of the huge Monsters, claws, teeth, tails flashing and whipping around.

I snatch the third book from Doris when she holds it up, but again nothing happens. "Okay, we need to leave and regroup," I agree and we back away.

That's when my world stands still for just a moment.

A tentacle comes whizzing in my direction, from a beast of the sea that is battling with Thrace to get to me. Its three eyes are fixed on me, a look of triumph in their aqua depths as the sharp tentacle aims directly for me. I feel it slam into me, the knife-edged tip burying itself deep into my chest, knocking me off my feet when it pulls back and a sucking wound, gurgling blood, forms between my breasts.

"Oh," I rasp, going numb everywhere except the agonizing pain from the stab wound.

"Thrace!" Doris screeches. "Kate's hurt!"

She drops to her knees next to me, slapping her hand over the hole in my chest as the battle rages on around us.

The noise fades to a distance. My vision goes gray. I know Doris is still next to me, trying to stop the bleeding, but my life's blood is spilling out all over the road.

Cries.

Tears.

Pain.

The sounds of war all around.

Howls.

Shrieks.

Agony.

Then...nothing.

* * *

"How is she?" A gentle, yet gruff voice echoes in my ears.

"Bad," another louder, harsher voice replies.

"How did this happen?"

"They came out of nowhere. Just appeared in the road and stormed towards her. I don't think this was intentional..."

I tune them out, trying to ascertain who is speaking, where I am, if I'm alive. I feel like a head with no body. There is no pain, but I know it's lurking. As soon as I move, it will hurt, so I stay still. The knowledge of what happened playing over and over in my head.

It *was* intentional.

That sea Monster's goal was to kill me, not claim me.

I try to speak.

I open my mouth, but my tongue is stuck to the roof. I choke, which turns into a cough, which inevitably brings the pain to a maximum level that is unbearable.

"Kate!" Doris exclaims, taking my hand. "Don't try to move."

"Too late," I croak. "Am I dead?"

"Nope, alive if a little skewered."

"Hmm."

"Does it hurt?"

I open my eyes finally, to give her a scathing glare. "No, I'm just peachy."

"Sorry," she mumbles. "I meant..."

"I know what you meant," I interrupt her. "Yes, it hurts. A lot."

"You were poisoned," Thrace says, swimming into view.

"By what?"

"Some sort of sea creature," he mutters. "I'm not really sure. Possibly made up."

"Great. So there's no antidote or whatever?"

"There is," Doris says, giving Thrace a weird look. "You don't need to know the ins and outs. You have been cured, but you will be sore for a while."

I chance a glance down at my chest. It is indeed healed, but why am I still so sore? I don't like it.

"This never should have happened," Eerie states. "What were you doing out there in the first place?"

His gentle tone from before has vanished and now he is pissed.

At me!

Why does the injured party get the wrath of the Monster?

"Trying to get the Monsters back in the books," I state, hauling my carcass into a sitting position. "We succeeded, until we didn't. Where did they come from?"

"Out of nowhere," Thrace says again. "They weren't there one second, and then they were. It was...odd."

"Do you think by putting some Monsters back, I brought out more?" I ask.

"No," Doris says. "I don't think so. They just appeared like the others. This wasn't your fault, Kate." She pats my hand firmly. I'm not sure whether to believe her or not, but there's no time for that.

"Did you kill them all?" I ask Thrace.

"Some. Eerie and the boys arrived and some of them ran. We needed to save you, so we don't know where they are, yet."

"Then we need to find them and send them back," I say

determinedly. "The plan hasn't changed. It's just grown a bit, that's all."

"Can you stand?" Doris asks.

I nod and swing my legs over the side of the bed. Luckily, Thrasher is there silently waiting to catch me when I fall. Which I do. My legs are like jelly.

"Maybe not quite yet," I mutter. He sweeps me into his arms, cradling me and I find a great deal of comfort from him.

Suddenly, this all gets too much, and I burst out crying, unleashing my frustration and upset over the whole situation.

"Oh, love," Doris says. "Let it out. You've been so strong. You deserve a good cry."

Sniffling into Thrasher's neck, I nod and accept the tissue that Thrace hands me. I wipe my eyes and when I remember that all eyes are on me, I get so embarrassed by my pity party, I cringe.

"Put me down," I say, squirming in Thrasher's arms.

"You sure?" he asks.

I nod.

He places me on my feet, and I grip his hand for support. How is it that some Monsters are monstrous, yet others can be so loving? I don't get it.

"That sea Monster tried to kill me," I state.

"Well, yes, but we think..."

"No, it *wanted* to kill me. I saw it in its eyes," I insist.

"Really?" Thrace murmurs. "Curious. The objective has changed with them. Why?"

I shrug. Who cares? I just want them gone from this world. All of them. I'm done with being scared and having neighbors run for their lives, only to be hunted down and eaten in my back garden.

"It's time to end this once and for all. I'm accepting my destiny, whatever the fuck that is. Doris, hand me my bag."

Wordlessly, she passes it to me.

I snatch it from her and open it roughly. I glare into it, taking in the contents, one by one, knowing that I have to do this. I have to be whoever my parents expected of me. And woe betide them, if they are still alive and living inside a book without me, I'm going to unleash a Monster the likes of which they have never seen before.

After I hug and kiss them and tell them how much I've missed them, of course.

Twenty-Six

Dainn

Something isn't right. Kate is pale and shaking. She is glaring into her big bag with concentration. I see her about to fall seconds before she does. I lunge forward to catch her, letting the bag drop to the floor as I catch her and scoop her up. Her head lolls back and her nose starts to bleed. The scent of it is tempting, but I would never taste her without her consent. It just seems wrong with her.

"Shit!" the old woman exclaims. I think her name is Doris. "What happened?"

I glance at Thrace, the worry etched on my face.

He is usually not that easy to read, but there is panic simmering under the surface of his cool exterior. "She is burning through the regeneration far quicker than I expected. I knew it wouldn't be permanent, but this is..." He gulps.

If Thrace is worried, then that means my own worry has just increased tenfold. I place her carefully on the bed.

"What do you mean?" I ask. "What do we need to do?"

"Give her more of your blood!" Doris screeches right next to my ear, making me wince.

"Of course I will, but that isn't going to help her for long," Thrace snaps, getting irritated but I can see it's only from concern.

"Just do it," Doris grits out, grabbing Thrace by his shirt front in a gesture that I can't help but snicker at. No one has ever dared to get in his face like that before. Except maybe Eerie.

She glares at me, and I shut it, the worry over Kate crashing back down.

We stand back and watch as Thrace slices his wrist open again and places it to her lips. Her wound is reopening slowly, oozing blood that has me mesmerized for a moment.

"It's not working. She's not ingesting enough," Thrace murmurs.

"Then how do we do this?" I ask, "There has to be a way."

"Can you drop your blood into the wound?" Thrasher asks, coming closer. He is anxious. I have never seen him so unsure of anything before, so it is a comfort to know that he isn't impervious to thinking about others and not just himself.

"Yes," Thrace mutters. "Yes, that might work."

Our eyes are riveted to the blood dripping into the hole in Kate's chest. She gasps, but doesn't wake up.

"It's working," he says. "But like I said before, this is not permanent. Only getting her out of this world and back to her own will."

"Her own," Doris says slowly. "You think that will work?"

Thrace nods and sits back after a few more moments. "See how she fares with this before I continue," he murmurs.

"Ekaterina is meant to be in our world, with us," I say, climbing on the bed with Kate. "She got locked out of our world when her parents were forced back into the book. There is only one chance for her to reopen the book, with the key that appeared when she turned thirty human years. Do you know where it is?" I ask Doris.

She shakes her head, but I get the feeling she is lying. "Kate needs to go home."

"Can we just wait for her to wake up before we do anything else," she says, sitting down on her other side and taking her hand.

"If you know where the key is, tell us now," Thrace demands.

"I don't. You need to ask Kate," she says shortly.

I place my head next to Kate's and sigh. I dislike the peace she is bringing me now. I should be focused on helping her, but all I can think about is how quiet it is in my head. Closing my eyes, I suddenly startle. Kate's thoughts are in my head.

"She is in pain," I blurt out, turning my face so that I'm touching her cheek. "Her soul is crying."

"What?" Eerie asks, having been silent for a while now.

"Oh, Kate," Doris whispers.

"We need to get her home NOW!" Thrace practically bellows.

"No!" Doris says, standing up. "Kate needs to fix this world before she goes anywhere. That's what she wants and the rest of us need. You can't leave us here with all of this!"

"Kate is in danger of losing her life," Thrace spits out.

"And so are the rest of us. I know Kate. She would want to stay and help *this* world."

"So, you do know where the key is, you just aren't going to give it to us," Thrasher says.

I tune out the arguing and focus on Kate. It's quiet in my head even though her thoughts are in there with mine. There is no chaos, just peace.

"Dainn!" Thrace snaps. "How are you connecting to her? Can you wake her up?"

I blink sleepily, having fallen into a bit of a daze with the silence in my mind. "I don't know. I thought you had a connection to her thoughts, anyway."

"Not while she is like this," he admits quietly. "How are you doing it?" I don't sense jealousy, which is strange, he is curious.

"It's not really her thoughts, more her *feelings*," I murmur, staring at her beautiful face. "She is in pain, but she can hear us and wants us to stop fighting. She agrees with Doris."

"Does she?" Thrace growls.

"Told you so," Doris snaps.

"All of this arguing is stressing her out," I say. "Please stop it. She needs time for Thrace's blood to work its way through her system. It's working. She feels stronger now."

"Then we wait and give her a bit more time. I will administer some more of my blood in a little while. In the meantime, Doris, if you know where the key is, you need to tell us. I give you my word that we will not leave until this mess is cleared up unless Kate's life absolutely depends on it."

Doris sighs. "I can't do that. It's for Kate to figure out."

"Figure out?" he asks, but again I close my eyes and leave them to it.

I curl up next to her and take her hand, kissing it softly. "Come back to us, Kate," I whisper. "We need you."

I fall into a light slumber, thinking about how strange this whole situation has been. Before we came out of the book, I had no memories of anything really. I knew I existed, I knew I was different to Thrasher, I know what we need to do and what is happening over in our world. The memories are implanted, or written, or whatever they are. I haven't experienced any of it. I don't know where we came from, but I know our purpose. Kate is our purpose. She is our mission. We need to take her home to save us all. We have fought to protect her and even though we failed, we will do everything we can to make sure she recovers from this. Then we can take her home to her parents and she can fix our world that is crumbling without her.

Twenty-Seven

Kate

I'm aware of my surroundings. I can hear everything they're saying, but I can't move, nor speak or even open my eyes. It's disconcerting to say the least. I have learned a couple of things though. My name is *Ekaterina*. It's pretty. Much better than boring old Kate. Wishing I could speak so I can back up Doris with Thrace, I inwardly sigh.

"Don't worry, pretty Kate. We will save you."

Dainn's voice inside my head makes me smile. He is sweet.

I feel him lean over me and press his lips to mine.

That's when my eyes fly open.

Staring into his green eyes, I smile for real and lift my head to kiss him again. "You woke me. It's like Sleeping Beauty."

"Huh?" he asks, scrunching up his nose.

"Nothing," I say with a giggle and sit up when he lets me.

"Kate," Doris says with relief. "How do you feel?"

"Like a Kate kebab, but I'll live. For now, I guess." Yeah, heard that bit too. I'm choosing to ignore it from here on out.

I've got work to do. Firstly, I stand up and grab Thrace by his shirt, pulling him towards me. Standing on my tiptoes, I plant a kiss on his lips that surprises him for all of a second before he wraps his arms around me and deepens the kiss.

"Jeez, get a room," Doris grumbles.

"We are in a room," Thrasher points out.

"Well, fuck this...I'm out," she replies.

I hear her march out and slam the door behind her.

Pulling away from Thrace, I say, "Thank you for giving me time to sort this out."

"Your life is mine to protect, my Queen. I will do anything and everything I can."

"Do you think she's gone?" Eerie asks, a lewd expression on his gorgeous face.

"Downstairs, at the very least," I smile.

"How do you feel?" he asks, with a hopeful note in his tone.

"Well enough to get the shit that needs to be done, done. The rest...it can wait until you take me home, back to my parents to save our world from being destroyed."

"How do you know about that?" Thrace asks, looking as disappointed as the rest of them that sex is not on the table right now.

I glance at Dainn. "Somehow, I can connect to Dainn. Our brains are wired the same, I think." He gives me a shy smile and takes my hand. His sharp claws rake against my skin, but I barely notice it. Maybe it is to do with the regeneration that Thrace's blood is causing. "But it's not important right now. Hand me my bag and ask Doris to come back."

Thrasher gives me my bag and Eerie reluctantly calls Doris back.

"No, nope, not coming up there unless you're all fully clothed. That includes you, dog-boy!" she shouts up the stairs.

Eerie's startled expression makes me laugh out loud.

"I don't have any clothes," he says.

"Here," Thrace says and snaps his fingers, clothing Eerie in sexy sweats and a vest that makes me want to rip them back off him.

"All clear," I call out and we wait for Doris to make her way back into the room. I give her a bright smile, even though the trepidation I'm feeling is clawing at my insides. I'm nervous, scared, hopeful, and a dozen other emotions that I can't name right now. Snapping my bag open again, I look inside and see not only the book, but also the big iron key. Without a word, I shut it, relief flooding me and making me slightly lightheaded. Believing in myself and believing who I am, has made this right. Doris knew what she was talking about. No surprise there. She seems very wise. I catch her eye and she gives me a knowing look with a secretive smile. She knows what I've seen.

"Let's go back to the library and round up the rest of the blank books. We have a town to clear up and a book world to save. Time is of the essence."

I don't need to add that my life is also on the line. I feel fine now, but I also know that Thrace's blood won't last for long. I must have this done before I collapse again. I have no idea why taking me back to the book world will save me, but if Thrace says so, then I trust him. I have to because the alternative is unthinkable. I'm not ready to bow out of life. Not now when I've actually started living it.

Thrace slips his hand into mine and with a snap of his fingers, we are back in the library, only we aren't alone.

All the Monsters have congregated here, which isn't really that unexpected.

"You find the books, we will keep them away from you," Thrace mutters as Eerie shifts into his huge demon dog form and the twins waste no time in going feral, launching themselves at the nearest creatures.

"Doris," I whisper. "Will you come back to my world with me, us?"

Her surprised expression makes me smile. She is pleased, but hesitant.

"You don't have to answer now. Just think about it. I don't want to lose you, just when I found you. Your friendship means more to me than..."

"Find the books, dammit!" Thrace yells at us, interrupting my heartfelt admission.

Doris snickers and takes my hand. "Let's do this and then we'll talk."

I nod and we skirt around the cluster of fighting Monsters to the Paranormal Romance section again. This time we scrabble through the books, yanking them off the shelves and checking for blank pages. If they have words, they get discarded. If they don't, I turn and try to make Monsters disappear. It's not seamless, but so far, I've managed to get rid of two Monsters with Doris's help. Unfortunately, the sea Monster that tried to kill me is still around and it's taking everything Thrace has not to eat him, by the looks of it.

"Just chomp on the fucker already!" Doris yells to him as wayward tentacles lash out our way again and we duck.

"Wait!" I shout out above the din of the battle. "Eeeek!" I shriek a second later, when I'm doused with blue goo that shoots out of the arm of one of the Monsters that Eerie decided he was eating, no matter what.

Doris's look of horror at my appearance, gives way to a snort of laughter that she can't control. It increases and bubbles up until eventually she is doubled over, slapping her thigh and choking on air, she is laughing so hard.

Standing there drenched in disgusting Monster parts, I huff out a breath when she stops enough to catch her breath. "If you are quite done, we are looking in the wrong section. We need Fantasy and Sci-Fi," I inform her haughtily and turn on my heel to stride over to the next stacks, wiping the gunk from my forehead that is threatening to slip down into my face, with as much dignity as I can muster.

Twenty-Eight

Kate

After the shock of being doused in goo dissipates, I quickly get to work on the books, pulling them out one by one. Doris, still chuckling away to herself, helps and soon we find a few to try.

I turn, holding one up at the beast who tried to kill me. He is currently wrapped up so tightly in Thrace's tentacles, it's like a BDSM party over there.

"Okay, you dick. I don't know why you wanted to kill me, but here you go back to your own world." I hold the book up and with Doris's hand on my wrist, I summon whatever it is inside me that does this. Bright white flashes of light come out of the book and sweep him up, squealing and whipping his tentacles everywhere. I belatedly hope that Thrace doesn't get caught up in the maelstrom, but it seems to only work on the real characters of the books.

"Don't think he wanted to go," Doris comments.

That's when the penny drops. "Duh," I say, rolling my

eyes. "That's why he tried to kill me. He didn't want to go back to the book. Maybe he dies in it?" I peer at the cover suspiciously. "Anyway, next!" I call out and it happens to be the one-armed blue goo Monster that Eerie took a bite out of.

Doris slaps another book into my hand. "Definitely this one."

"Yep." It's on the cover, albeit with *two* arms.

Once again, I hold it out and the creature swirls around and gets sucked into the book, along with the other two Monsters remaining.

"A few of them ran," Thrasher says.

"Great," I mutter and rub my fist absently in between my breasts. There is a weird tingle and only when Doris pats my shoulder, do I remember that is where the hole is supposed to be. Thrace's blood must be wearing off again.

"This is exhausting," I comment suddenly.

"Take a break, love," Doris says kindly. "Go and have a lie down in your office."

I nod and without another word stumble towards the office, I wash up as best I can in the small sink over on the far side and then flop down on the small couch in the corner. I know I have work to do to clear these Monsters and get back to my own world – whatever that is – to heal myself but I can't even lift my head right now. My eyes close and I feel the lull of slumber fall over me.

I'm running through a beautiful green forest. Laughing and twirling, enjoying myself more in this moment than I think I ever have. I turn, smiling to see my parents grinning at me, watching me. I look up to see a huge fairytale castle in the distance, my home, and I run towards it, only to trip up seconds later.

I cry out, falling to the soft, green ground, but it prickles my skin as I touch it. The green grass has turned black and the trees all around me are dying. A briar has wrapped itself around my ankle, which is what tripped me up, the thorns digging into my skin, making me bleed. Frantically, I look around and see dead vines, inching up the trees, entwining around them, choking the life out of them. The dead leaves fall to the ground and crumble to dust as they hit the blackened forest carpet. I shiver in the sudden cold.

My parents start crying, blurring out of view.

I cry out, reaching for them, but the briars are restraining my wrists, wrapping around my throat, pinning me to the ground. I scream...

The sound of hushed voices rouses me. I feel like I've been hit by a truck. Blinking my fuzzy eyes to focus my vision, I take in Thrace, Eerie, Thrasher and Dainn, all with me in the small office, talking about...something. Arguing, even.

"Where's Doris?" I slur, wishing for some water.

They stop talking and look over at me.

"She was tired, so I took her back to your home," Thrace says.

I frown. "Is she okay?" I ask, sitting up.

"She is perfectly fine. You have been asleep for hours, so she decided to get some rest as well."

"Okay," I say. I place my hands either side of me on the couch and hoist myself up. My head spins, but it's short-lived. I feel much better now, the nightmare notwithstanding. That place was creepy and horrible. Thrace must've given me more of his blood because I feel just fine.

Walking over to the office door, I reach for the handle, but one of Thrace's tentacles wraps around my wrist, reminding me of the briars. I pause and look back over my shoulder. Another tentacle circles my other wrist, and he turns me to face him, pushing me gently up against the door.

"Kate," he says softly. "There is something I need to share with you."

I lick my lips nervously. This doesn't sound good. "What is it? You don't need to restrain me to tell me something."

"I have a fantasy of you," he says in the tone that washes over me and soothes my growing nerves.

"Now isn't the time," I murmur.

"The need to impregnate you consumes me, Kate. You have been mine since the day you were born. I have been waiting until the day I could claim you and make you mine." He moves a little bit closer, another appendage gently stroking my face. "We are meant to be together, Kate and I cannot wait any longer to see my fantasy come to life."

"What?" I ask, slightly confused by what he is saying. His words are all lilting together, all I can really hear is the cadence and it's making my brain fuzzy, but in a good way.

"I want to fuck you, Kate, until I come inside you and my seed implants in your womb. I want you to grow my child within you. The thought of it arouses me to the point where I feel like I'm going to burst if I don't see it through."

In the blink of an eye, he is in my personal space and unzipping his pants. His huge cock springs free, making my mouth water at the sight of it. Timing be damned. I want him.

I feel my shoes being removed and then my sweats are drawn down, all by Thrace's tentacles. The tip of one of them shoots straight up my pussy as he restrains my ankles. I gasp and then moan as the appendage bends up and starts to rub my clit.

I should be doing something else. I can't remember what it is, but I know this isn't it. I want to do this, but there is something more important to be dealt with first.

My knees buckle as the pleasure races through me, but

Thrace holds me up, plastering my hands up high above my head and pulling my legs wider apart as he lifts me off the ground slightly. He fucks me slowly with his Kraken appendage and it doesn't take long for me to climax, coming all over his tentacle with a loud cry of release.

"Oh, Kate," he murmurs, "feeling you tighten around me, makes me want to come inside you."

"Please," I cry out, my eyes tightly closed. "Fuck me, Thrace. I need to feel you."

"He is, Kate," Eerie's soft voice sounds in my ear.

I open my eyes and look down but all I see is the sea-green tentacle still thrusting inside me. "No," I shake my head. "I want to feel your cock inside me."

"Shh," Thrace hushes me and rubs my clit harder.

I cry out and my breath hitches when I feel him vibrate inside me.

"Let me bury my seed inside you, Kate. Allow me to impregnate you as the burning desire is demanding me to do."

"Wait," I mutter as his words sink in. "Wait...I'm not..."

He groans loudly and I feel him come inside me. My gaze drops to his cock in shock. It isn't inside me, so does that mean...?

"Aah," I cry out as the vibrating increases all through my body and makes me come again.

"That's it, Kate. Accept my seed. Take it inside you. Nourish it. Grow a child, our child..." He inhales sharply and then removes the tentacles from my pussy and clit. I feel the cum sliding back out, but then he is there, pressing his body against mine, his cock at my entrance.

"Do you want this, Kate?" he asks, the soothing tone rippling over my skin, making it tingle. "Do you want to have my child?"

"Yes," I cry out and then scream when he thrusts his

massive cock inside me, the suckers on the underside, suckling at the walls of my pussy.

It feels like the top of my head is about to blow off with the pleasure that is coursing through me. I close my eyes again as Thrace fucks me against the door of my office. Eerie's fingers lightly trace over my hip, all the way down to my clit. He circles it slowly, so slowly, nuzzling at my neck in a delicious way that I need to continue.

"Do you know what is happening, Kate?" Thrace whispers to me.

"Yes," I pant.

"I need to hear you say it."

"We're fucking," I rasp.

"More than that, my Queen. We are mating. Do you understand?"

My eyes fly open as full understanding hits me. His words from earlier that I felt the need to respond to, sink in. It is something that I never imagined, never thought I wanted. God knows, I never had anyone to think about it with. But all of a sudden, the thought of him impregnating me is turning me on. My nerves ping and zing and all the blood rushes straight to my clit, where Eerie's fingers are teasing it. I come in a shudder of pure ecstasy.

"Yes!" I cry out. "I understand. I need you, Thrace. I need all of you. You are mine."

"Princess," Eerie pants in my ear. "Say that again."

"You are mine!"

With a noise of desire, he slides his finger from my clit to shove inside my pussy with Thrace's cock.

"You are ours, my Queen," Thrace groans, one of his tentacles wrapping tightly around my waist. "You are mine and you are theirs."

He lets out a grunt and thrusts deeply, coming inside me with his cock this time and my banks burst. My pussy soaks his cock to the point where it slides out on his next thrust. I squirt all over Eerie's hand.

He groans softly in my ear "Fuck, yes, Kate. You are so sexy. I need to feel your pussy around my cock."

"Yes," I pant, still held up by Thrace's tentacles.

He moves out of the way and Eerie's hands go around my waist. Thrace lets me go completely and I drop slightly, but Eerie tightens his grip. The twins move forward on either side of me and shred my hoodie and top with their claws until it drops off me. Leaning down to bite and suck my nipples, I throw my head back, wrapping my legs around Eerie. He guides his cock inside my drenched pussy with a feral noise that thrills me to my core.

"Perfect," he whispers. "You are perfect. A true warrior, a true Queen. You will make a wonderful mother, Kate."

"Ah," I cry out, as once again the thought of conceiving a child out of this union excites me.

Eerie fucks me roughly in the middle of my office as the twin Monsters bite me, piercing my flesh and lapping at my blood. A tail comes up to rub against my clit. It's not enough. It's never enough with them.

"More," I pant. "I need more."

Eerie walks us over to the desk and pulls me off his cock. He turns me around and bends me over. His fingers find my rear hole and I squeak.

"I didn't mean..."

"Shhh," he soothes me. "Just feel, Kate."

His other hand drives into my pussy, scooping up enough cum to lube up my ass.

"Oh, fuck," I moan when he inserts a finger gently into me. I have never done this before. I don't think I want to now, but I forget all about being prim and proper and just...feel.

Twenty-Nine

Eerie

Sliding my cum-coated middle finger gently into Kate's ass is a pleasure that I have never known before. I have wanted to claim her this way since the day I first saw her. I can tell she has never done this before, so I go slowly, preparing her as best I can.

The twins are practically drooling all over her to get to her pussy, but they will have to wait.

Once I think she is ready, I remove my finger and take her hand, leading her over to the couch. I sit down and pull her onto my lap. Lifting her up a little bit, I position my cock at her rear hole and push it slowly inside her.

She yelps, but I keep going, not giving her the chance to back out of it. Before she knows what's hit her, Thrasher is in front of her with his two cocks, ready to shove into her pussy at the first opportunity. I draw Kate back, so she is lying on my chest and Thrasher lifts her legs up. I thrust deeper into her ass with a groan of pure satisfaction.

"Oh, yes, Princess. You feel so tight, so good."

"Ah!" she screams as I invade her where no male has taken her before.

The honor is all mine, and I will cherish taking her anal virginity forever.

Thrasher leans in and guides his double cock into her pussy, gripping her ankles tightly. "Fuck, yes," he rasps. "You're so wet, oh, yes."

Kate whimpers as three cocks start to hammer into her, claiming her, filling her up until she can't stand anymore and climaxes heavily, screaming until she is hoarse.

Dainn grips her by her throat as she quietens down and presses his lips to hers. He kisses her, biting her lips until she bleeds, but she doesn't complain. She takes it and then when he presses his double cock to her mouth, she opens wider and sucks the tip of both of them into her filthy, pretty mouth.

I meet Thrace's gaze when he sits on the arm of the sofa to watch this ravaging of his Queen. He is aroused, but not by us. Just by her. She is being spectacularly fucked in all her holes with more cocks than she can realistically handle, and yet she begs for more.

With a grunt of triumph, I come in her ass, shooting my load and releasing some of my frustration at being trapped in this world.

I lift her up and let my cock slide out of her hole, shuffling over to make way for Dainn to take my place while Thrace holds her up with one of his appendages.

"Are you ready for him, my Queen?" Thrace asks.

"Yes," she pants. "Yes, fuck my ass hard."

"Oh, Kate," Dainn mutters, fisting her hair and pulling her head back so he can graze his sharp teeth over her neck. He crams his two dicks into her small rear hole, tearing her and making her cry out, but she doesn't stop him. She wants us all, every which way we can take her.

"I love you," I whisper against her lips, leaning over her before I kiss her.

Her eyes light up, but she has no breath to speak. She is panting raggedly, but she is loving every second of this. Thrasher groans through his release and Dainn follows not long after as Kate comes again and again.

"You are spectacularly full of cum, aren't you, dirty Kate," I murmur.

She gasps but then smiles, slow and sexy with a wicked edge. "Taste it," she says, shoving my head in between her legs.

Slightly shocked by her demand, but no less willing to do it, I lap at the creampie dripping out of her pussy, tasting the cum on my tongue as I fuck her with it. She squirms closer, fucking my face with her pussy, grinding against me, eager to make herself climax once more. I help her out by taking her clit between my teeth and tugging on it roughly, flicking it with the tip of my tongue until she cries out, weak and exhausted.

"Rest now," Thrace murmurs, taking her in his arms and transporting her to her home, so she can sleep in her own bed.

I reluctantly watch them go, wishing that I could go with them, but if I do, I won't let her rest. I will just keep riding her until she is nothing but a limp rag doll in my arms.

"Do you think Thrace did it?" Thrasher asks quietly.

"Yes, I'm sure he did, but if he didn't, he will try again soon."

I'm not sure how I feel about her having a child with Thrace. I didn't really think about it before now. I hope one day she will be able to have mine.

That is if we can get home and fix the plague that is sweeping across our land. Soon.

Thirty

Kate

Still slightly dazed by the events that occurred in my office, I feel thoroughly fucked. Probably because I *was* thoroughly fucked. All over. In all my holes. Many times.

I stand there with a towel wrapped around me as Thrace runs me a bath.

"Let me know when the temperature is right," he says. "I like it cold, but I think you will skin me if I give you a cold bath."

I giggle, suddenly a bit shy. I bring the towel up to cover half my face and I look down at my feet. I dip my hand in the bath water and draw back with a hiss.

"Too hot," I complain.

Thrace turns on the cold tap more and soon we have the perfect temperature.

"Did you mean what you said?" I blurt out as he helps me climb in.

"Every word. But did you have something specific in mind for me to reiterate?"

Damn him. Am I that transparent?

"Yes."

"And?"

"Does it really turn you on thinking about getting me pregnant?" I ask, glad the water is on the hotter side so my warm cheeks can be attributed to that.

"Very much so," he replies and sits on the edge of the bath. "Is that okay with you?"

I nod slowly and settle back, relishing the warmth as it eases my aches and pains.

"Does it turn you on?" he murmurs huskily.

"It did," I reply carefully. "I haven't thought much about having children. I never wanted to put them through what I went through. Not to mention, I've never had anyone to imagine that life with."

"Until now."

You have to admire his confidence.

"Until now," I mutter.

"Do you regret what we did?"

"No," I say quickly. "It was sudden, but I'm...happy."

"I'm glad. I'm happy too."

He picks up the sponge and starts to wash me gently.

"And the other stuff? What you said about being mine since I was born?"

"What about it?"

"How did that happen? How old are you? Did my parents give me to you?" I bite my lip as the questions come thick and fast.

He smiles. "Yes, they did. I don't actually know how old I am. I came into creation some time ago. Memories are... different with me, with us. I have only really started to make real ones since I came here, I think."

"Oh," I whisper, a bit confused. But I suppose it makes sense. If he came out of a book, it must be a little bit strange. "And my parents?"

"Their existence is a mystery. You will have to ask them when you see them again."

"Why didn't they come for me? Why did they go in the first place?"

"They are trapped in our world, Kate. The world is being destroyed, a plague is sweeping through it, killing off almost everything. We need to get you back where you belong to restore the balance."

He looks very concerned about that.

"So I was born there?"

He nods. "Yes. You were in danger when you were born. That's why your parents brought you here. But losing you has sent our world into a tailspin. Your parents tried to bring you back five years ago, but instead it took them and without you there, they're trapped."

"So what does that make me?" I ask, even more confused.

"Our Queen," he replies. "The key to fixing everything."

"*I'm* the key?"

He nods slowly. "There is a symbol. An actual key. Within it lies the power, *your* power to take us home and repair the damage that has been done by your absence."

"Why was I in danger?" I have to keep asking questions. I need to know. I have to understand because right now, I'm fucked if any of this makes sense.

"There are Monsters who wish to harm you. Who wish to claim you, but to do their bidding. I was given the honor of being your future mate and was sent here to retrieve you and to mate with you."

"What about the others?" I frown. Surely my parents didn't send them all to *mate* with me?

"Eerie and I have been involved since I can remember. It

143

was written that way, I suppose. Don't take that the wrong way. I care for him," he adds hastily. "But you are my heart. You chose them to be with you, Kate, so who am I to argue?" He gives me a soft smile.

"What do you mean I chose them?"

"The day we ravaged you in this very house. You invited all of them to share your body. That was your choice, Kate. Not mine or anyone else's."

"Oh," I say, enjoying that sense of power for a moment. "Thrace?"

"Yes, Kate."

"I think I'm falling for you."

"I'm glad, Kate, because I know I love you."

"Will you make love to me?" I ask tentatively. We have only ever fucked. I want it to be *more* next time. "Just the two of us?"

His blue gaze penetrates mine.

"Will the others mind?" I suddenly worry.

He chuckles softly. "No, they won't mind. They know you are mine. And to answer your question, I would be honored to make love to you, Kate. I want to take you in my arms and give you the love you deserve."

I swallow and nod. "Afterwards, will you tell me more about...*me*?"

"Anything you want to know. You were supposed to figure all of this out yourself, but I am done watching you struggle. I need you to know how powerful you are, what a goddess you are. Even more so than we thought."

"Goddess? I thought I was a Queen?" I snort at that, but then remember what Annabelle said and some of the other Monsters.

"You are nothing less than a goddess, Ekaterina."

I give him a slow smile and stand up. He wraps the towel

around me and helps me out of the bath, smoking us to my bedroom.

"Do you think Doris is okay?" I ask suddenly.

"I'm sure she is fine, fast asleep. We can check on her after I take you to bed."

He takes me in his arms, and presses his lips to mine, claiming my mouth in a sweet, sweet kiss. It feels so right. There is nowhere else I want to be right now. I feel safe, beautiful, powerful and most of all, loved.

Thirty-One

Thrace

Sweeping my tongue over Kate's is like everything I ever thought it would be. Perfect. She is mine in every single way and now she knows it. She will grow my child inside of her and I will cherish every moment of my life with her and our family.

She lets the towel drop and I step back to worship her body. I fall to my knees and kiss her stomach, hoping that I impregnated her earlier.

"Are you sure you want to do this?" I ask.

She nods, running her hand through my hair. "I'm okay. If we didn't conceive before, I need us to try again right now."

My dick goes hard at her words. "You have no idea what you are doing to me, Kate." I close my eyes and rest my forehead against her.

"Breed with me," she whispers, which makes me snap my head up to stare into her beautiful face.

"Oh, fuck, Kate," I groan. "Say it again."

"Thrace, I want you to breed with me. I want to mate with you and make your baby."

"Uhn," I groan and slide my finger over her clit.

She moans and throws her head back.

"Sore?"

"No, it's perfect."

That's all I need. If she didn't want me to touch her, she would say so. I stand and pick her up by her hips, dropping her lightly on the bed. I stand over her, opening her legs before I duck down and kiss her pussy before I thrust my tongue into her. She arches her back, murmuring my name. I fuck her with my tongue, tasting her deliciousness until she comes against my mouth. Her clit is still engorged and sensitive from earlier, so the merest flick of it excites her.

"Thrace," she breathes, writhing on the bed, pushing her pussy closer to my face.

"I love you, Ekaterina," I whisper and stand up, stripping my clothes off with just a thought. This power has been given to me by her parents, the authors, the *creators* of our land, to protect her as best I can. Her gaze hungrily takes in my cock, and it bounces under her admiration.

She lifts her hips and I drop down on top of her, leveraging myself so that I don't squash her.

"You are a goddess," I whisper before I kiss her again. "I am so aroused by the thought of coming inside you, of making you pregnant with my child."

"Take me, Thrace. Release inside my pussy, make a baby with me."

"Fuuuuuck," I groan and slip my cock inside her.

She rasps as the suckers attach themselves over her g-spot and massage it to the point where she screams and shudders uncontrollably in my arms.

"Yes!" she cries out. "More!"

I ravage her then.

Slamming my hips against hers, burying my cock as deep into her as her body will allow, I ride her until my cold blood heats up and races through my veins until I'm lightheaded.

She meets my thrusts, full-on but then I remember what she wanted, and I slow down.

She moans in protest, but I shush her with a kiss.

"Slow, Kate, slow. Revel in my touch, in my cock sliding in out of your pussy, my lips pressed against yours."

Kate arches her back, pressing her breasts closer to me.

I drop my mouth to her nipple and suck it gently until it is a hard peak that I want to bite, but I don't. I don't want to hurt her at all during this moment she has entrusted me with. I shuffle us further up the bed and then roll over, so she is on top. I want to watch her ride me. I want to give her all the power. She balances her hands on my chest as she rotates her hips and then rocks back and forth. I feel myself on the verge of coming, but I hold back until she is ready for me.

"Are you ready to come inside me?" she purrs.

"Yes," I pant like a fool.

"I'm ready to drench your cock."

"Oh, Kate." I grip her hips tightly, holding her still so that I can thrust up into her high and deep, making her moan.

"Come for me, my Queen. Let me see in those pretty eyes how my cock makes you feel."

"Ah!" she cries out and convulses as the climax hits her. She clenches around my cock, and I unload my cum into her, flooding her body with my seed.

"I love you, Ekaterina," I whisper.

"I love you too," she whispers back and collapses on my chest.

I gather her to me and pull the covers over us. She is asleep within seconds, and I tighten my hold on her, never wanting to let her go. I stroke her hair and kiss her, in complete awe of the woman who will bring all of my fantasies to life. She is strong, beautiful and humble. She will serve us well as our Queen and I can't wait to return her to our home and spend the rest of my life making her happy.

Thirty-Two

Kate

I'm running through a beautiful green forest. Laughing and twirling, enjoying myself more in this moment than I think I ever have. I turn, smiling to see my parents grinning at me, watching me. I look up to see a huge fairytale castle in the distance, my home, and I run towards it, only to trip up seconds later.

I cry out, falling to the soft, green ground, but it prickles my skin as I touch it. The green grass has turned black and the trees all around me are dying. A briar has wrapped itself around my ankle, which is what tripped me up, the thorns digging into my skin, making me bleed. Frantically, I look around and see dead vines, inching up the trees, entwining around them, choking the life out of them. The dead leaves fall to the ground and crumble to dust as they hit the blackened forest carpet. I shiver in the sudden cold.

I know I've seen this before now. This isn't the first time, or the second.

My parents start crying, blurring out of view.

I cry out, reaching for them, but the briars are restraining my wrists, wrapping around my throat, pinning me to the ground. I scream.

A Monster looms over me.

An enormous black beast that is made entirely of smoke.

He roars in my face, and I shriek again.

A child's scream fills my ears.

My *scream.*

I struggle against the briars, the thorns digging further into my skin as the sky turns smoggy. I can't breathe. The air is cloistered and fetid.

Rotting.

Everything is rotting around me.

"You are coming with me!" the Monster rumbles, reaching out for me.

Its hand clamps around my neck and squeezes tightly, somehow corporeal, yet misty at the same time.

I squirm and kick out, but the briars wrap even tighter around me.

My eyes fly open as I struggle for breath.

The black smoke Monster from my nightmare is looming over me, its hand around my neck.

I squeak, looking frantically for Thrace, but he is bound up tightly in a coil of smoke that has his arms pinned to his sides, unable to help me.

The Monster hauls me out of bed, dangling me from its fist.

"Queen," it rumbles in a voice so dark, so frightening, I start to tremble.

"Kate!" Thrace yells, straining against the smoky lasso swathed around him.

I scrunch my eyes shut, hoping that I'm still in my nightmare, but it becomes apparent that the nightmare is in fact, reality. Memories of something that happened to me long ago. I don't remember. In the last dream, I was maybe three or four. Somehow, I must've got away and I'm guessing my parents brought me here to *this* world to keep me safe. All of these thoughts are processed within the space of about two seconds. I open my eyes again, knowing this is the beast that Thrace told me about.

"I will have you this time," the Monster's thick voice echoes around the room.

"No!" I choke out and struggle in its grip.

Its hand closes around my neck even tighter and I start to panic, but then I try to calm myself. Panicking will get us nowhere.

Thrace is yelling at me, but I tune out his words as I think of a way to remove myself from this hold.

"Kill him," the Monster intones to the smoke bind wrapped around my lover.

"Thrace," I rasp, fear coursing through me now as I see the smoke choking him, claiming his life. "No!" I won't lose him. Not now. Not after everything. I fling my hand out, my other one going to my neck to try to loosen the Monster's grip.

I squeak in shock as white smoke, just like Thrace's, shoots from my hand engulfing him and the black smoke, and then he just...disappears.

"Fuck," I croak. What did I do? Where did I send him? I kick out at the beast, hoping to connect with some other corporeal part of him, but it seems it's just its hand.

Its smile turns feral, chilling me to the bone.

"No one is here to save you now, Queen," he grits out.

He brings me closer to him and licks my face with his smokey tongue.

"Eurgh!" I shudder, wishing that I wasn't quite so naked, dangling here from its fist.

In an instant, I'm clothed.

Again, Thrace's smoky power wafts around me and I'm dressed in sweats and a hoodie.

The Monster grunts, disappointed that I'm now covered up.

"Help," I croak when he flattens me to the bed, his intent very clear on what he is about to do.

I scrunch my eyes up again and fling my hand out, "Help!" I rasp, my voice hoarse and bruised from being choked.

"Kate!"

The relief floods through me when I hear Eerie's voice. I brought him to me. Along with the twins.

The Monster roars in my face and drags me back up, my feet barely touching the ground as he faces the three furious Monsters. *My* furious three Monsters.

Eerie's eyes have gone wild and in the next second he has burst into his massive demon dog form, in my bedroom, knocking the dresser and causing it to shake madly.

The sheet that covers the mirror slides away, and I gasp when I see a purple and white vortex swirling on the surface of the glass.

A screech of unheard of decibels emanates from the vortex.

"Aah!" I cry out, clapping my hands over my ears at the same time I hear Dainn cry out.

He drops to the floor and curls up, keening and trying to cover up his ears. Thrasher glances at the vortex and then reaches for the sheet, flinging it over the mirror before he drops to Dainn's side and strokes his back, a look of fear on his face for his twin who is writhing around, grunting with agony.

Eerie launches forward, teeth bared, and he crashes into the smoke Monster who has become corporeal, somehow, maybe from the vortex. It lets me go, flinging me into the en-suite. I land hard on my back with an, "Ooof," hoping that Doris is okay and has fled the scene for her own safety.

"Kate!" Thrasher cries over the din of Dainn and the fight. "Use your power."

"I don't have any!" I yell back, getting to my knees, my hands still clapped over my ears.

"You brought us here!" he shouts. "Do it! Send it away!"

I bring my hands down to stare at them. I have no idea where this power has come from, nor if I can use it again. Without thinking, I throw my hand out towards the mirror and the smoke coils through the air, hitting the sheet and frying it before it smashes into the glass, breaking the mirror.

The smoke Monster screams.

I watch in horror as it is sucked into the mirror, into the vortex.

"You can't escape me for long, Queen!" it bellows before all goes quiet.

The mirror returns to normal, Dainn quietens down and Eerie shifts back to his human form.

I lick my lips, nerves pinging all over the place.

"Where is Thrace?" I whisper.

"Right here," he says from behind me.

I turn to see him and Doris in the doorway. Doris is gaping at me like she's seen a ghost.

"Where did you go?" I stammer.

"Just outside," he says with a smile. "You need to get a handle on that power of yours, my Queen. And soon."

"Mine? It's yours," I mutter, confused as all fuck as the last few minutes sink in.

"No, Kate. It is ours." He strides over and drops to his knees, grasping my hips as he kisses my belly.

Staring at him in shock, I whisper, "Already?"

He nods, grinning up at me. "Already, Kate. You are with child as it was meant to be."

Thirty-Three

Kate

The feelings overwhelm me. I don't know quite how to process this. How does one give birth to a baby Kraken? A half Kraken, half whatever I am, anyway. I cup Thrace's face and kiss his forehead before I turn from him with a worried glance down at Dainn.

I drop to my knees next to him and cradle his head in my lap.

"What's wrong with him?" Thrasher asks quietly.

"There is nothing wrong with him," I murmur. "He is different, that's all. Special."

"How so?"

"I don't know."

"He is a key," Doris says, coming closer.

We all look up at her.

"What do you mean?" I ask.

"Like you," Doris replies. "I don't know if he unlocks, or locks, but he is sensitive to the portal."

I stare into his face, contorted with the agony the vortex caused him. "Does it still hurt?" I whisper, stroking his face.

He shakes his head and opens his eyes. "No, not now that you are next to me."

"Two halves. You unlock, he locks," Doris states.

"How do you know any of this?" I inquire.

She shrugs. "Just seems obvious to this old bird. I could be wrong."

"No, I don't think you are," Thrace murmurs, shuffling forward and taking Dainn's hand in his. "He and Kate are definitely connected on the same wavelength, and Kate is the key to opening our world."

I purse my lips together and then lean down to kiss Dainn on his mouth before I pull back. "I think it is time to go home."

"Couldn't agree more," Eerie mutters.

"What about all the Monsters here?" Doris asks.

I meet her gaze. "We will fix that. I think I know a quicker way to get them all back home in one fell swoop. We need to get them all to the library," I say, standing up and walking over to the dresser. I can still hear the hum from the mirror. Snatching it up, I hand it to Thrace, who has also risen. "Take this to the library. Doris and I will follow shortly."

He nods and disappears, taking the others with him.

I turn and face Doris, arms folded. "You know more than you are letting on, don't you?"

"Not at all, just observant and distanced from this situation," she says.

"Humph," I mutter. "Then why do you amplify my power?"

"I'm guessing because you felt you needed help, so you projected that onto me."

"Jesus," I snap at her. "You have an answer for everything, don't you?"

She gives me a sassy smile. "So, your plan? You are going to open up one big portal?"

"Yes, and throw the books inside. I'm hoping the Monsters get sucked up into the portal and then into their respective books."

"It could work," Doris says with a nod. "Worth a try."

"Yes, exactly. Right now, I need to get home and find out why my world, my *real* world, is dying."

"Let's go then."

"Will you come with me?"

She pauses. "What makes you think I even can?"

"If I'm supposed to be this Book Goddess person then I'm assuming if I want you to, you can."

"Confident," she says. "I like it."

"So you'll come?"

"We'll see."

I guess that's all I'm going to get from her, so I drop it for now.

"Do you think you can...smoke us to the library?" Doris asks, just as I was wondering the same thing.

"I'm going to try," I say with a shaky smile.

I hold my hand out and she slaps her palm against mine with an encouraging nod. Closing my eyes, I picture the library and then when I hear Doris's gasp, I open them again.

"Getting good at that," she says with a wink and turns from me to start gathering up all the books.

As in *all* of them.

"Not taking any chances?" I laugh.

"Nope," she says, throwing them to me.

"What will happen to the library?" I catch the books and pile them up next to the mirror.

"Hopefully, once all the Monsters are returned to where they should be, this world just goes back to normal."

"That's taking a big leap of faith."

"I believe in you."

I give her a hesitant smile. I wish I had her faith in me.

"Ready?" Thrace asks.

He has placed the mirror on the counter.

"Think so. Dainn? I need you to touch the mirror," I say, going to him and placing my hand on his arm. "Can you do that?"

He nods, his face showing his anguish over my ask.

"It will be okay. I'll be here," I reassure him with words that I don't really feel.

I gesture for Thrace to remove the sheet from the mirror. I briefly see my reflection, but this time instead of shying away from it, I stare into my own eyes. I can see a difference in my whole demeanor. My eyes are sparkling, and it seems that I don't even need my glasses anymore. I haven't worn them since all of this started, yet my vision is perfect. My hair is shining, and my posture is confident and upright. I smile at myself and then I flick my gaze to Dainn. "Are you ready?"

He nods briefly and lifts his hand to the left side of the mirror, placing his fingertips to the glass.

With a look back at Doris to give me the confidence boost I need; I reach out and touch the other side of the mirror.

The shriek of a portal opening makes me wince.

Dainn stifles his grunt of pain, but I meet his gaze and smile.

He smiles back, showing me his sharp teeth, letting me know he is okay.

The vortex swirls around the pane.

I lean down to pick up the first book and with a sharp intake of breath, I throw the book into the mirror and then step back with a squeak of surprise as a gust of air rushes out of the portal, and bursts through the library doors.

Thirty-Four

Kate

Encouraged by this, I throw the next book in and then the next. More tunnels of wind, funnel out of the portal and head off to, presumably, find the appropriate Monsters. That is confirmed when we start to see the gusts return to us, sucking a variety of Monsters into the mirror. I speed up, throwing in two, three at a time as Thrace hands them to me. It spits out the ones it doesn't want and soon we have gathered up every single Monster from the town, except the ones that are with me.

"Just two more books," Doris says, handing me the one I read that brought *my* Monsters to life, plus the one my parents came out of in the first place. Then she passes me the old iron key and I stare at it, wondering what I'm supposed to do with it. I place it inside the Monsters book and close it, hoping that is enough.

I jiggle them in my hand. "You coming?"

"Why not?" she says with a shrug. "There isn't anything here for me anymore."

"You sure?"

"Yes," she says with more conviction. "Yes, I'll come with you."

I grin at her and chuck the books and key into the portal. Then, taking Dainn's hand and Doris's in my other, I lead us into the vortex that opened up to let us in.

It's like walking through fog. I have no idea what is going to appear on the other side.

I know everyone has followed me in. I can hear their footsteps behind me. I keep moving forward. My stomach is in knots. I feel slightly sick with the anxiety of what awaits us on the other side. What if that massive smoke Monster is there, mouth wide open, ready to gobble us up and spit out our bones?

That theory is squashed though, when the fog thins and we step out onto dead, black grass in the middle of the dying forest. I gasp at the horror of the land around me.

Letting go of Doris and Dainn, I look around, my hand on my stomach. There are tall, dead trees all around us. The clearing we are standing in is a black ring of nothingness. There is a deathly silence all around us.

"This is horrible," I murmur.

"This is why we need you to fix it," Thrace whispers, keeping his voice low.

I understand his need for keeping as quiet as possible. A threat could loom at any moment.

"How?" I whisper back, pain and anguish coursing through me.

"We need to close the portal," Dainn interrupts.

"According to the wise one, over here, that's your job," I whisper.

"Both of us," he says and holds his hand out for me to take.

He links our fingers together and kisses the back of my hand. "Do you know what you're doing?"

"No clue," he replies. "But with you by my side, I can't fail."

"You're sweet," I murmur and look back at the swirling fog we emerged from moments earlier. I hold my hand up and he does the same. Touching our fingertips to the fog, we let off a spark of electricity that burns our skin against the dampness of the mist.

I hiss and pull my hand back; he does the same.

We watch as the fog swirls up into a funnel and then disappears completely, leaving us in the gloomy, eerie, desolate, dead forest filled with trepidation and angst.

"We should find your parents," Thrace whispers urgently, taking my hand again and pulling me away from where the portal closed.

"Good idea," Doris murmurs.

"You okay?" I ask, bumping her shoulder with mine as she falls into step beside me.

"I'll live," she replies, looking all around. "This is not how I pictured it."

"This is from my nightmares. Ever since I was a little girl, I dreamed of this place," I say, looking over my head and shivering at the chilling sight. "I only realized it was a memory when the black smoke Monster was in my room earlier..."

"Rathnor," Thrace interrupts.

"Hmm?"

"His name is Rathnor. He is the Monster that wanted to take you as a child and groom you to be his puppet when you became Queen."

"Ugh!" I exclaim and then shush myself, waving my hand

about as I give Thrace a sheepish look. "Any idea how we get rid of him?"

"If we knew that, he wouldn't still be here," Thrace points out, rather reasonably.

"Of course," I mutter.

"Where is the castle?" Doris asks quietly.

"About a mile walk from here. You used to be able to see it, but with the descent of the darkened sky, it is now impossible."

"Are my parents definitely there? They haven't really died, or anything have they?"

"They are there."

"Why did they make me think they'd died in a car crash? Why not just tell me the truth?"

"The truth is, they did die in that crash. In a manner of speaking," he explains. "It was as your father was driving over to your house that they were sucked back into this world. The spell your mother cast, intending you to be with them when the portal opened, somehow set off too early, so you weren't with them. The car crashed and burned, and no bodies were recovered."

I frown at that. How is it that I never pressed to see their bodies? I was in shock, practically catatonic, and was told they were burned beyond recognition. I just let it slide right on by and now that I think about it, the officer I spoke to seemed kind of shady.

This whole situation is just shady as fuck, and I hope my parents can explain their actions to me in a way that appeases the stress and grief this has all caused me.

Continuing on in silence, Thrace and Doris on either side of me, with the twins and Eerie behind me, I suddenly feel a jolt of something familiar.

Familiar and comforting.

A feeling of true recognition of this place made up of nightmares and blocked memories.

I stop dead in my tracks, causing Thrace to jolt to a halt two steps in front of me because he is still holding my hand.

I turn to Doris, anger bubbling up.

She faces me with a raised eyebrow. "What is it?"

"You!" I hiss, jabbing my finger in her face. "I remember you. You deceitful old bat!"

She gives me a shocked look, but then she just rolls her eyes and shrugs. "About time, Princess. I was beginning to think you'd never remember your dear, old Aunt."

Thirty-Five

Kate

"Aunt?" I spit out, not caring now about the volume. "Aunt? What the hell? All this time? What? What? Jesus!" I stamp my foot and drag my hand out of Thrace's so that I can fold my arms over my chest, to show her I mean business.

"Your father's sister," she informs. "Years after you left, I was assigned to follow. When your parents went to the other world to protect you and to make sure you were safe, they needed me if anything happened to them. No, they didn't know something would happen. It was a failsafe," she says, cutting me off at the pass. "I was forbidden to discuss this with you, to even really associate with you in case your memories of me came back. Rathnor forced their hand into making a decision to send you away until you were old enough to come back and rule the land as you were meant to. The spell to return you on your twenty-fifth birthday went badly. It misfired, as Thrace said, pulling your parents back into this world without you. And without you, the key, they are trapped."

164

"You lied to me," I hiss, so unbelievably pissed off with her, I want to cry and curl up in a ball. "All this time. All the pain I was in over my parents' death. *Supposed* death, and you just let me grieve."

"I had to. I had a mission and telling you about all of this wasn't it. I did what your parents asked of me. They made me swear on a script of my own death that no matter what happened, I would leave you to figure this all out on your own. To force you into trying to open up the world before you were ready, would've ended in disaster for you and for them and for all of us. The world would've crumpled in on itself, and you would've died."

"You don't know that!" I shriek. "I'm stronger than I look."

"Oh, I know that, love," she replies. "But what good am I to you dead? If I'd told you, I would've been killed by the promise I made and broke. I barely got away with what I told you about the book," she adds with an annoyed look *at me*.

"Dammit!" I scream at her, tears pouring out of my eyes and streaming down my cheeks. "Damn you! Damn them!"

I am distraught.

Beyond distraught.

Utterly *broken* by this information dump that has severely fucked with my head.

I moan, gripping the sides of my face, my fingernails digging painfully into my cheeks.

"Don't," Doris says, desperately.

"Is Doris even your fucking name?" I shriek at her.

"Actually, yes," she replies.

"Humph," I mutter and then turn on Thrace. "Did you know this?"

He shakes his head. "No, there was no mention of a chaperone."

"Because it was a *secret*!" Doris yells, suddenly as agitated as I am. "I'm sorry, Kate. I really am, but you have to under-stand the position your father, both of your parents put me in."

"And Harold?" I barrel on, ignoring her. "Did he even exist?"

"Yes," she hisses. "He is alive and well, right here in this land, waiting for me to return to him."

"So you just left him here? For Twenty years?"

"I had no choice."

"All those photos of you in your house?" I scramble to try and remember if I've ever seen Harold. I come up empty. I really have been walking around with my head up my ass and blinders on.

"They are from here. We age differently here, Kate. I'm older than I look." She purses her lips at me. "Don't even go there."

"Well, fucking fuck!" I bellow in her face. "You really are a piece of work, you know that?"

"You can be angry with me all you like, but I did what I had to, and I was here for you when you needed me, to guide you through this process. You can't deny that, Kate. You know I'm right. You know that there isn't anything I wouldn't do for you, and keeping you safe from yourself was paramount to my mission."

"Argh!" I cry out and spin, my hand on my hip, the other on my forehead.

The Monsters are all silent. Probably not wanting to get in the middle of this, whatever the fuck it is...family business?

"We really should keep going," she says eventually.

"Oh, to the castle that you have no idea where it is," I snarl.

She shrugs. "Seemed like something I would ask if I'd never been here before."

"Grrrr," I growl, but then the laughter bubbles up. I choke

on air as I snort hysterically. Everyone leaves me to my mini meltdown, but then Doris joins in my laughter.

"I know how all of this sounds, Kate. I really do," she says in between bouts of mirth. "I'm sorry for my part in it."

My hilarity dies down and I glare at her. "Doesn't sound like you had much choice. My parents have a lot to answer for."

She sighs. "Do you forgive me?"

"I'm not sure there is anything to forgive. Of course you had to abide by what they wanted if your life was on the line. I just can't believe that they would do something so cruel."

"It wasn't out of cruelty," she says defending them. "They needed to make sure that *you* were safe and that was all they were thinking about. I wanted to do the same thing. I still do. You are my niece, Ekaterina. I love you."

Her heartfelt statement thaws the ice that had built up between us. But she broke my trust and that is going to be hard to repair.

"We are not okay," I say quietly. "I understand, but everything you have done and said has been to deceive me."

"I know," she says sadly. "I wish things could've been different."

"Me too."

"Will you at least try to forgive me, in time?"

I nod briefly, trying not to cry. My emotions are on overload right now.

I frown at Thrace suddenly. "Why are we *walking* to the castle? Can't we just smoke there?"

He shakes his head, coming closer again now that it seems safe to do so. "With the world dying as it is, there is no magick, Kate." He waves his hand around and a pfft of smoke puffs out but dies instantly.

"You try?" Doris asks carefully.

I wave my hand like Thrace did, but nothing. Not even a pfft.

Great.

"Walking, it is then," I mutter and turn, heading back in the direction that we were going before I remembered who Doris was.

Silently, we leave the forest and pass by a massive lake. The water is dark and bubbling up, steam drifting off the surface in a haunting scene that will be hard to forget.

"Your home?" I ask Thrace.

He nods sadly. "Used to be," he replies shortly.

We pause and mourn the loss of the land that I remember from the beginning of my nightmare.

"And this is because I left?" I ask after a moment, the guilt rushing over me and taking my breath away.

"It is because Rathnor wanted to change the story," Eerie snarls suddenly, startling me after being silent for so long.

I turn to look at him and then blink when a small furry head pops up out of his hoodie he is wearing. I smile and reach out to pet the little dog. "You made a friend?"

He shrugs and shoves the dog back down.

"How did you smuggle him through the portal?"

"Thrace gave him to me as we entered, along with the clothes," he says gruffly, not happy to be caught out caring for the fluffy creature.

"You are sweet," I say and rise up on my toes to kiss him.

He appears pleased, but then with a sharp inhalation, his face goes dark.

"Rathnor," he mutters viciously and turns around, keeping me behind him.

Thirty-Six

Eerie

Facing off with the Death Monster is not what I wanted to do today, but here we are. I know I need to shift, but there is something making that very difficult. It's only when I notice the thin stream of black smoke encircling me, that I become aware of the issue.

Rathnor is clouding my mind and my ability to shift.

It pisses me off.

Then he does something so repulsive, I want to rip him to shreds.

His trail of smoke grabs my pup and sucks him up into the quagmire that he is, eating him whole.

"You fucking dick!" I snarl and shake off the dampening cloud of smoke as he just laughs at me.

I shift in a burst of fur and claws. It hurts like fuck for about a second, but then I launch myself at him, skidding right through the foul smoke, choking on the sulfurous smell.

"Eerie!" Kate calls out, panic in her voice.

I grimace inwardly. She should know not to worry about me. Now she has drawn attention to herself.

It only occurs to me a second later, that I fell right into Rathnor's trap. I was standing in his way, and he effectively got rid of me so he could get to Kate.

Growling viciously, I lunge through Rathnor again and knock Kate off her feet, standing over her so that Rathnor will have to go through me to get to her. Thrace has already shifted, and the twins have gone feral, crouched low, ready to pounce.

"Queen!" Rathnor rumbles. "You coming here has saved me the work of breaking free again. I thank you for making this easy."

A tendril of smoke wafts through me and reaches her. She scrambles out of the way, rolling on the ground until she is clear to get to her feet.

"You want me, Smokey?" she goads. "Come and get me!"

She turns and runs in the direction of the castle, which surprisingly swims into view, the closer she gets to it. She is healing the land, the longer she is here.

Kate!

If she heard me, she's ignoring me. I pounce forward, getting in between her and Rathnor, who has taken her invitation to heart and followed her.

I have no idea what she is planning on doing, but she has practically stopped my heart with this bravery. This *stupidity*.

Kate!

Kate!

Ekaterina!

This time I know she heard me, but she is definitely ignoring me. The trouble with Rathnor is, he is only corporeal when he wants to be. Stopping him is impossible.

I growl and snarl at him, but he pursues Kate, drifting right on by me, Thrace and the twins.

Pushing aside my guilt over the little pup that I promised to protect, I lumber after Rathnor, with the others right behind me. Doris has taken off after Kate and is surprisingly keeping up with her.

Seeing her grab Kate's hand and pull her to a stop to yell something at her, I see them turn to face Rathnor. Kate holds up her hand and my heart nearly stops. She has no magick. Even if she did, she doesn't know how to use it properly, or how to wield it correctly.

Rathnor has reached them and with a maniacal laugh, which chills the blood in my veins, he whisks Kate up in the smoke and drags her off. Doris clings to her for dear life, but she isn't strong enough and Rathnor doesn't want her. He severs the grip, by twirling a coil of smoke around Doris's wrist and yanking back, snapping her arm.

She screams, but out of fear for Kate. I can *feel* it.

No! Kate!

I've got this.

Three words that she projects into my head which stop me cold. This was her plan.

What is she thinking?

I turn to Thrace, dread and fear in my gaze. He returns it, cursing and shifting to his Kraken form to follow them. I don't hesitate to follow. Saving Kate now is the only option, even if it means dying ourselves in order to do it.

Thirty-Seven

Kate

Twisting around in the tornado of black smoke, I feel nauseous, but hold onto the contents of my stomach as best I can. Although vomiting all over his insides does sound appealing, the fact that it'll get all over me as well, is not.

Sucked further into the darkness, I feel cold, and I feel nothing but hatred and the need for power.

It is black as night inside the Monster as we travel quickly over the land, to who knows where. His lair probably. He has to have a lair; I mean, come on. Name me a villain in a book who doesn't have a lair.

Wishing for a moment that I had Annabelle and Mr. War with me, I feel something soft on my hand and then it licks me. I yank my hand back, clutching it to my chest, my heart pounding with fright. But the soft yap that follows informs me that it is no threat.

"Hey, cutie," I murmur, picking up the small dog that Eerie seems to have adopted. He sits on my lap and licks my face. "Glad to see you made it. But this isn't over. When I make my move, run away as fast as you can. Can you do that?"

He replies with a soft bark and climbs off my lap, ready for action.

"Alright, Rathdick, where are you taking me?" I mutter.

"Nowhere you can escape from," he replies from all around me and then I'm dumped out of the smoke machine. I only just have reflexes quick enough to grab the dog as well on my way out of the worst ejection seat in history.

"Oof," I groan when my back hits the cold stone ground that is hard as fuck. Obviously. It's stone. And ground. "Bastard," I mutter, rolling onto my side so I can get to my knees quickly.

I appear to be in some sort of dungeon. I'm not surprised. It lacks originality and there are very few evil creatures that have an original flare that makes them interesting instead of boring as fuck.

"Bo-ring!" I sing-song in an irritating voice that belies my inner fear. I'm practically shitting myself because I have no clue what I'm supposed to do now. All I knew was that I had to get Rathdick away from everyone else before he killed them trying to get to me.

"Silence!" he roars, getting right in my face. "You are nothing but a puppet, young Queen. You will sit on the throne, but you will do my bidding. I will rule this land in darkness and fear. Everyone will cower before me..."

"Oh, for fuck's sake..." I interrupt him with an eyeroll. "You have nothing new, do you?"

"What?" he asks in a relatively normal tone as I cut off his evil rant.

It is so unexpected; I can't help but snort in his face with nervous mirth.

"See?" I choke out. "You aren't scary. You're just a normal, old Monster."

"Normal?" he hisses. "I am Death, I am your worst nightmare, I am..."

"Yeah, yeah. Look, Smokey. I'm not interested in doing your bidding. In fact, it is the last thing I want to do. You aren't going to kill me, because you want me, so...impasse? I'd say so." My hands are on my hips and I'm giving him my best stern Librarian's glare.

To my shock, he gives me an abashed glance. "You are a very frustrating creature," he sniffs.

"And you are...I don't know...what are you?"

"I just told you. You should cower before me."

"Yeah, not gonna happen." I wave my hand around, knowing the magick is all around me now. I can feel it coursing through me, making me stronger, making me light-headed but in a good way. The white smoke swirls up from the ground, forming a whirlwind. It is small to start with but then it heightens in its intensity. Whipping around and around, I swirl my hand in a bigger circle.

"You can't defeat me, *Queen*," Rathnor spits out, back to the asshole Monster we know and hate. "You aren't strong enough."

"You'd like to think so, wouldn't you...but...I'm a really quick learner."

As the funnel of smoke gets bigger and bigger, enveloping us all in its path, I unleash every ounce of strength I have into it and push out with a loud scream.

His shriek as it catches him and knocks him back, echoes around the cavern. The small dog starts barking, but I'm nowhere near done with this thing yet.

Nor is it done with me.

Our banter time is over.

He lashes out with his black smoke, and it clashes with mine, making a choking gray smog that is drawing all the air out of the dungeon.

The dog stops barking and makes a choking sound, but I have to ignore it. All my focus has to be on defeating this Monster.

"You have done nothing but cause torment and agony to this land!" I shriek, pushing back against the black smoke. "Tearing me from my home, my parents, everything that I was meant to be!"

I take a step forward, but I stumble. The power surge is taking more of a toll on me than I realized.

Rathnor laughs at my weakness. "You can't defeat me!" he roars. "I will sap your strength and then I will take your power, locking you inside your own head so you can do my bidding."

"Never!" I bellow, the wind of the magick whipping my hair into my face, into my mouth making me gag slightly. I don't have the hands to remove it. I need both of mine to push back against the black smog.

"Kate!" Dainn's voice comes out of nowhere, somewhere, all around.

"I've got this!" I grit out.

"Your life force is draining."

I don't think he is in the cavern with us. But I can hear him.

I choose to ignore him.

Doubling my efforts, the sweat drips down my forehead as I battle with this Monster.

Exhaustion sets in as I keep him just out of reach, but I can't hold it much longer. He is going to beat me. He is going to win and there is nothing I can do to stop it.

Thirty-Eight

Dainn

"She is dying," I mutter, trying to get back into her head, but she has shut me out. Or is too tired to open up the channel to allow me in.

"No!" Thrace bellows in my face. "Do you know where she is?"

"Why don't *you* know?" I ask, my hand on my head. The noise is back and it's getting louder and louder with each passing second.

"I can't reach her. If I could, I would, dickhead," he growls.

"Now, hang on a minute," Thrasher jumps to my defense for the first time, ever, it seems. "Don't blame him for your failure."

I tune out the argument that follows, closing my eyes and trying to concentrate enough to figure out where Kate is.

Then it hits me.

I see through her eyes. She is crying with pain and frustration. She is losing the battle. We need to get to her.

"Where are you?" I mutter.

I can hear a dog in the background, making a weird noise that's halfway between a choke and a bark.

"Eerie. Your furball is alive and with her. Can you connect to it somehow?" I murmur, not sure if I'm loud enough for him to hear me, but I can't increase the volume for fear of breaking my own head.

"I'll try," he whispers.

Opening my eyes, I watch him focus. He shifts and with a grunt, he heads off in the direction Rathnor took Kate.

"Thrasher, Thrace, come," I say, as I pass them, still arguing.

They go quiet and once they realize that Eerie might be on the trail, they fall into step behind me.

"Is he tracking Kate?" Thrasher asks.

I shake my head. "The furball."

"Huh," Thrace mutters. "Ingenious plan. Canine to canine."

I don't bother informing them it was my idea. What would be the point? Especially if we don't get to Kate quick enough. As we amble along behind Eerie, I try to focus on her again. I feel a hand on my arm and look down.

"Doris. Are you okay?"

"Don't worry about me, all healed," she replies, shaking her arm around. "Kate is fixing the land, the magick, just by being here."

I nod, knowing this is true.

"Where is she?" a voice suddenly thunders all around us and then Enrico and Josefina appear in front of Eerie. "Ekaterina?"

They look all around for her, but no one wants to tell them that Rathnor took her.

"Doris!" Josefina screeches. "Where is she?"

"Rathnor has her. She is..." Doris starts, but trails off when Josefina starts wailing and turns to her husband for comfort.

The emotions are running high and deep. It affects my soul, making it ache and cry out for relief, for it all to just stop so I can think.

"Eerie is looking for her," Thrace states. "Let us return to our search."

His completely dismissive tone as he strides confidently past them, shocks them. I rush after him and even Doris ignores them, rejoining the party on the hunt for Kate.

Eerie rumbles low and dark, letting us know he has them. He must've picked up Kate's scent.

He races forward at speeds we are unable to keep up with but try.

Over boulders, under low hanging trees, we keep moving forward, witnessing the rebirth of the land that Kate is healing.

I reconnect with her then. She is wailing, her soul attaching itself to mine, crying out for help. It urges me forward faster until we see the giant opening of a cave carved out into the big mountain that rests in the Northern part of the land.

"Wait!" Thrace says, holding up his hand. "If we rush in there, we might fail her, or worse."

"She knows we are here," I say, eyes closed. "She says stay away. She needs to focus."

"We aren't leaving her to die in there," Thrasher snaps.

I open my eyes and smile at him, taking his hand. I reach for Thrace. He snaps his tentacles around my wrist and wraps another around Eerie, instinctively aware of what I need him to do. "Knowing we are here is giving her the strength she needs," I say quietly and draw on the power of the three

Monsters that I'm connected to through blood and through Kate. I channel it up and out, and then driving it down, locking onto Kate deep below us, under the surface of the soil. "She isn't dying," I murmur. "She is killing him."

Thirty-Nine

Kate

"You can't take away the one thing that I have," I shout to Rathnor as he tries to suck all the life, all the good, all the positive energy out of me. "You can't take away my love."

"Love," he grits out. "Love is nothing!"

I stumble back, but I *will not* go down. Not now. Not ever.

"Wrong! Love is everything. I have it, you don't and that is what is going to be your ending!" I close my eyes and lower my hands. I don't need to see this. I don't need the action of pushing the magick towards Rathnor.

All I need is me.

Well, and the Monsters outside that have my back. They love me. I love them. It's unfathomable to think that I could love the creatures from your worst nightmares. That I could love them in such a short space of time.

But I do.

I love them.

I know they love me. It is what is seeing me through this. I was convinced I was going to lose. I was seconds away from giving up, exhausted, mentally and physically. Almost on my knees.

Then I felt their presence all around me. Dainn connected to me in my mind, letting me know that they are all there waiting for me to end this and bring life and love back to the land that we are all from. Nothing else matters.

The grief over losing my parents will never go away, but it is dulled, dimmed by the light all around me. It doesn't matter anymore. I'm not interested in hearing a rehash, or excuses and explanations of what happened. It's done. It's over and I'm moving on from it. A fresh start.

I gasp as I see the golden light through my closed eyes, blinding Rathnor and stifling his darkness, removing his shadows from the cavern.

I forgive my parents for leaving me in that moment.

I forgive Doris for her betrayal.

It will take me a minute to get back to where we were, but we will. I have absolute faith in that. Just as I have absolute faith in what I have to do now.

"Your reign of terror over this land is ending," I tell Rathnor. "Your time is up. You will never torment anyone ever again."

I open my eyes to see that my white smoke is now golden and wrapped around Rathnor, smothering him. He is choking, dying, being snuffed out.

The air clears of the stench from evil and death.

The small dog with no name starts yapping again and I bend down to scoop him up.

"You didn't leave me," I murmur, kissing the top of his head. "You are a brave little pup and Eerie will be so proud of you."

He licks my nose and I giggle.

"What can we call you?" I murmur as the golden glow dies down, twirling around as Rathnor disperses from existence, surrounded by light and love.

Drawing in a deep breath, I look around and see the mouth of the cavern. I march towards it, needing to get out of here and back to the creatures who love me, back to my parents.

Moments later, I see the light from the cave entrance, and I stumble out into the sunlight, green grass and trees swaying in the warm gentle breeze. I see everyone gathered, waiting for me. I place the pup carefully on the ground before my parents rush to me, flinging their arms around me, telling me how much they love me.

I take it all in before I step back and give them a sad smile. "I missed you," I say. "You left me, made me think that you were dead. I grieved for you for five years. Five years, and now you are here in front of me, alive and well. And I'm glad. I really am. But I can't do this. I am not a Queen. I'm not the daughter you want me to be. I'm just...me." I shrug and with every single ounce of strength that I have left in me, I lean forward and kiss them both, before I walk away, leaving them to stare after me, calling my name.

Ekaterina.

"And my name is Kate," I say, even though I know none of them heard me. "My name is Kate."

Forty

Thrasher

We all stand stock still, watching Kate walk away from us.

"Erm," I mutter, wondering if we are supposed to go after her or stay where we are. I look to Dainn for the first time, ever for help.

He smiles and lopes after her like a joyous Monsterling, which spurs me forward, followed by Thrace and Eerie.

"Kate!" Josefina shouts out. "Stop. Where are you going? You can't leave! You belong here!"

She ignores them.

I pick up my pace as the small furball runs next to me, Eerie galloping along still shifted. His tail flicks out and wraps around Kate's waist, lifting her up mid-run to place on his back. She laughs with joy and grips his fur as he heads for the forest. He knows exactly where she wants to go.

We all know.

But how will we fit into her world? It's not going to be easy, but I know that we will try.

"Wait up!" Doris calls out, struggling to keep up.

"You're coming back?" I ask, slowing down.

"You bet I am. But this time, Harold is coming with me." She turns to look in the distance where a man is standing on the horizon. "Tell Kate to wait for me, please," she says.

"I'll tell her, but I'm not responsible for her actions."

She nods and rushes off towards the man.

"Kate!" I call up to her as we run past the blue lake, shimmering in the sunlight. "Wait!"

She turns, her face filled with laughter and happiness. She says something to Eerie and he stops, crouching down, so she can slide off his back. She runs to me and flings her arms around me. Laughing, I scoop her off her feet and twirl her around.

"Are you sure about this?" I ask, placing her back on her feet.

"More than anything, ever," she says. "This place is amazing, it's gorgeous and the fact that my parents created it, wrote this world and it came to life is something that I won't be able to fully understand for a while. But all my memories are slowly returning. I was not happy here as a child, knowing my future was all mapped out for me."

"You absolutely do not have to stay now that Rathnor is defeated," I say, "but what about us?" I have to ask.

She smiles and cups my face, her palm soft against my rough skin. "I want you to come back to *my* world with me. I know things will be strange there for you, but I know that I can't stay here."

I look back over the landscape that is both familiar and yet strange at the same time. Our memories are all a swirl of what is real and what has been written. I vaguely remember being in the book that Kate read, but I know it wasn't real. Not really real. It was a creation by the same authors who made this world. Looking back at Kate, I take her hand and kiss it. "Nothing could stop me from wanting to be with you."

"Same goes for all of us," Thrace says. "You are still carrying my child and there is no force in any world that could stop me from being with you."

She smiles. "That makes me happy."

"Doris also wants to come back," I tell her. "She went to get Harold."

Kate giggles. "Good, I was hoping she would. We have some repairing to do, but I couldn't have done any of this without her, or you."

I sweep her into my arms and kiss her, biting her lips gently with my sharp teeth.

She pulls back and turns towards the forest. "Let's go then," she says.

I would follow her to the ends of any world and back. I'm so glad that she decided we were worth taking a chance on.

Forty-One

Kate

We enter the clearing to find that my parents are already waiting for us.

"Kate, you can't go back. You belong here," my mom says.

I go to her and stroke her face. "No," I say. "I belong back in my world. This life you want for me, isn't for me. I don't want it. I have defeated the Monster as I was supposed to do, and that's it. I'm done. You can stay or come, whichever, it's up to you...but that's the point. It's up to you, just as my life is up to me. If you choose to stay, I will come and visit, or you can visit me. I'd rather you came back with us, in time, so we can rebuild our relationship, but I'm not staying here to do it."

Mom stares at me, her eyes filling with tears. "We are so proud of you, Kate. You have grown into such an amazing woman. You deserve to live the life you want."

She hugs me fiercely and I return it.

I turn to my dad. He looks like he wants to argue with me,

but I smile and take him in my arms as well. "This world you created is beautiful, and there are plenty of creatures here who can now enjoy it and live their lives again. My memories are returning the longer I'm here. I know you are the authors who built all of this. I know that I have this gift of bringing worlds to life. But all I want is to go home and carry on as I was, only this time with love and happiness."

"You should," Mom says, wiping tears from her eyes. "We want you to stay, but if you can't, then we have to let you go. We will visit once full order is restored here."

I nod and squeeze her hand before I let it go. I'm not telling her about the baby Kraken growing inside me. I want to keep that a secret a little while longer. Who knows if they will turn around and kill Thrace, or if they will try to keep me from leaving?

That's the thing now.

I just don't know.

Taking Dainn's hand, we walk over to the place where the portal opened earlier. We reach out, prepared to see it shimmer into view.

I knew it would, but it still makes me jump a little bit and laugh nervously.

"Kate! Kate!"

I turn to see Doris rushing into the clearing with a man I recognize from the photos as Harold.

"Is there room for us to return?" she asks hesitantly.

"Of course," I say with a smile.

"Are you sure?"

"Shut up and jump through the portal," I say.

I watch her and Harold go and then Eerie, back in human form, with his dog in his arms, steps forward, Thrasher next and then Thrace takes my other hand and leads me to the swirling vortex with Dainn.

I smile at my parents, knowing that this isn't the end. I will see them again very soon. I grieved for them for so long, but now I know that they are alive and well and living the lives they want to. What more could I ask for? Right now, I need them here so that I can begin to navigate my way through being involved with four Monsters and having a Monster baby.

Turning my gaze away, I look up at Thrace and give him a nod to let him know I'm ready.

He steps through, drawing me and Dainn with him and we arrive back in the library where all is calm and peaceful and as it was meant to be.

"One thing," I say, as I pull away from Dainn and Thrace to fling the sheet back over the mirror. No way am I ever looking in that thing again. I'll just have to buy a new one. Turning back to the Monsters, I add, "No more eating the townspeople."

"Then what are we supposed to eat?" Thrasher asks, concern all over his face.

"Raw steak from the butcher, for a start," I inform him.

"Oh," he says, looking disappointed, but I'm not budging. "Fine," he grouses after a few seconds of hesitation.

"Good," I say and then turn to Eerie. "You going to name him?"

He shrugs. "What am I supposed to call him?"

"He was really brave in the face of Rathnor. The calm in the storm."

"Then he shall be called Stormy," Eerie declares.

"Good name," I say with a smile and ruffle his ears before I turn to Thrace. He smiles, slow and sexy and I melt.

"I love you," I murmur, when he wraps his arms around me. "All of you. It was knowing this, that kept me going."

"You are incredible," he whispers. "I am so excited to be here with you, and to create memories with you and our family."

Turning in his arms to take in our family, the Monsters, the beings that have gone from terrifying to beautiful, the woman who has gone from elderly neighbor to best friend, the feeling of happiness, something that has long since been out of my reach, falls all around me. I thank my parents for writing my destiny the way they did so that I got to meet them all, but mostly, I thank them for having the strength to let me go and make my own way in the world. Even if it isn't the one they wrote about.

Thanks for reading!

If you want to find out if War really has a 13-inch cock, click this link for the completed Demon Queen Monster RH series! Hell's Belle

Join my Facebook Reader Group for more info on my

latest books and backlist: Sinfully Delicious Romance Reader Group

Join my newsletter for exclusive news, giveaways and competitions: Eve's RH Newsletter

Excerpt from Hell's Belle

A year and half ago

Annabelle

I fluff out my vivid red hair and adjust my huge tits in the black leather bustier. Leaning in closer to the mirror, I pucker up and apply a coat of red lip gloss to my full lips. I wink at myself, my green eyes alight with admiration. I know I'm gorgeous. I don't even have to adjust anything about myself, even though I could.

"Happy birthday, Sis," my twin brother, Shax says, lounging in my doorway, tapping his fingers on his thigh. He is dressed head to toe in black which makes his light blond hair look even brighter.

"Baby," I cry at him and fling my arms around him. "One year today, I will rule Hell! Fucking can't come soon enough."

He grunts at me. He hates it when I call him 'Baby'. He was born before me, or should I say, *my* dad, with the help of *his* dad, pulled him out of our mother before me. It was positioning, nothing more, but he prefers to think he's my older brother. My precious twin by some twist of celestial fate where we have different fathers. I would die without him. We are inseparable.

He loops his arm through mine. "You will kick ass," he says, telling me what I want to hear, when I want to hear it as he always does. He props up my ego and I adore him for it. Not that I require validation, I know I will kick ass, but it's nice to hear as well.

I bend down and pick up Babe, my nail studded bat, that is leaning against the wall by the door. "Time for the Daily Dealings. You in?"

"Not today," he mutters. "Watching you deal with the disobedient Demons in this place, while a delight, isn't on my birthday wish list."

"Oh?" I inquire, now full of curiosity. "Who is the lucky female?"

He rolls his eyes at me. "Wouldn't you like to know," he drawls.

"Yes, that's why I'm asking," I reply with a tut.

"Go and do your thing, Belle. I'll catch up with you later." He leans forward to give me a kiss on my cheek.

I pout at him but let him go.

"Ready?" Dad asks me, flaming in beside me with a broad grin. He is the Devil and he indulges my evil side with a fatherly delight.

"Always," I say. "Do we have some really bad Demons on the docket today?"

"As it is your birthday, I ensured that there were," he says with a laugh, but then he goes serious. "You are carving out your destiny, Annabelle. I couldn't be prouder of you. We have one year left to make sure that when you take my power to rule Hell, you are ready."

I frown at him, the thrill I had dissipating quickly. "What do you mean 'take'?" I ask him carefully. He has never mentioned 'take' before. I assumed he would hand it over and I'd be the Demon Queen.

He sighs and takes my hand. "I can't give it to you. It's something you have to take. You have to be prepared to do whatever you need to do to take it."

"What?" I snap at him. "Don't be ridiculous." What he is suggesting is out of the question. "I am not fighting you for it."

"You'll have no choice," he says.

"We will find another way," Mom says, slipping in next to Dad and fixing him with that glare that makes even the most powerful Demons quake in their boots. The self-appointed Queen of Hell is a delicate, small blonde female. But looks can be deceiving. "I told you, I will find another way," she adds.

He bends down to kiss her. "And just in case you don't, Annabelle needs to know what is required of her to rule," he says.

I look between the two of them, my anger flaring up. "Way to ruin my fucking birthday. Thanks a lot," I snarl and march away, pissed off and scared at what my father wants me to do. I cannot leave it to my mother alone to find another way for me to get that power. I'm going to have to help her because one thing is damn sure, in a year's time, I'm becoming Queen. I just don't want to have to kill my father to do it.

Present day

Annabelle

My eyes fly open.

I wriggle on the black satin sheets of my bed and then look down.

I sigh.

"What are you doing?" I ask the Demon that is tongue fucking me – not that well, I might add.

He stops and looks up. "Uhm..." He has absolutely no idea what to say.

"One nighter means one night," I inform him, bending my knee so that I can push him away from me with my foot. "It's not that hard."

"I—I'm sorry, Your Majesty," he stammers and scrambles off the bed.

"Get out," I grumble as he fumbles with his clothes.

He runs naked out of the room as my pet Hellhound, Musmortus, growls at him from the corner, her three heads snapping their jaws, eager for a bite of Demon ass.

"Good girl," I murmur to her and sigh as I climb off the bed and stretch.

I walk over to the glass wall on the far side of the room that looks out over the den of iniquity several floors down on the ground. All of the rooms in my new residence look out over the entertainment area.

I smile as I watch my minions. Each one has been hand-picked by me to provide the fun I do so enjoy watching. The Seven Deadly Sins in action, all day every day. It sends a shiver down my spine and peaks my nipples, exciting me way more than the little Demon had with his tongue up my cunt only moments ago.

I'm past this. I want more, but I *need* more than any one Demon can give me. For starters, my sex drive is too high for only one Demon to keep up with up. But it is more than that. I haven't found a single male that can handle *all* of me. I know I'm high maintenance in every way and I totally know that I have anger issues. It is something that I'm trying to work on.

I hear the door, that the Demon had left wide open, close quietly and then a warm body presses himself against me.

"Drescal," I murmur as his hands come around to pinch my pebbled nipples before he nuzzles my neck, brushing his lips lightly over my skin.

"Anna," he croons.

My blood tingles. He has a slight accent which makes him pronounce my name *Ahna*. I enjoy it far more than I would like to.

My body responds to him, warming up at his touch.

He dips his hand lower, gliding over my clit before he slips a finger inside me.

"You know that my pussy is already full of Demon cum," I whisper wickedly.

He withdraws his finger and pushes me gently up against the window, my huge tits squashing against the glass for everyone to see, if they look up.

"I'd be disappointed if it wasn't," he whispers in my ear before he nips my lobe and then licks my neck.

My breath catches and I spin around, taking him in.

He is the stereotypical tall, dark and handsome. Although, 'handsome' doesn't really cut it. He is gorgeous. His dark hair flops over his forehead, making my hand itch to brush it back. He towers over me, his dark eyes sweeping over my face as I give him a once-over that I know will make his cock hard.

I part my lips, staring at his and he leans down to delve his tongue into my mouth in a sensual kiss that makes my knees weak. He is good at seduction. It's his damned job. He is an Incubus. His powers don't work on me – I'm immune to all Hell-ish powers. The heat between us is natural and as much as I want to explore it, I'm afraid that if I do, he will come up short and then this fire will die.

He wraps his arms around me as I kiss him back and he walks us over to the bed. He pushes me down gently, stripping off his black duster, his eyes hot with desire. He starts to unbutton his black shirt, but I stop him from taking it off.

"Leave it on," I order him.

He narrows his eyes at me but does as I ask. He knows now this is a hard and fast fuck and nothing more. He swiftly undoes his black pants and they drop around his ankles.

I fall back and part my legs. "No need for foreplay," I state. "I'm already well-lubed."

He snorts. "Oh, Anna," he murmurs. "How many Demons did it take to make you come last night?"

"Too many," I sigh. "How many females did you seduce last night to make *you* come?"

He chuckles, ignoring my question. He leans over me, bracing himself. I wrap my legs around him, pulling him closer. He wastes no time in thrusting deep inside me. I arch my back and cry out softly.

He knows how to get this done. He makes me orgasm like no other male ever has. He knows it, he uses it to keep coming back and I let him because the high I feel when the climax tears through my body from his long, hard strokes is something that I cannot recreate, not for lack of trying.

"Yes," I pant. He hits my G-spot and the tingle in my blood from his nearness sets alight. "Fuck, Dres, that's it, baby!"

He grunts and fucks me harder.

I dig my sharp, black-lacquered nails into his back as I squeeze him with my thighs, riding the high that he's bringing to me even before I come.

"Anna," he moans, pulling all the way out and then slamming back inside me with such force, the bed rocks. "You drive me wild."

"Ah!" I scream as my climax hits me hard. My blood roars through my body, my nipples are aching they are so erect, my clit pulses as my pussy clenches around his enormous cock.

"Fuck, yes," he mutters and then he pounds me one last time before his own orgasm explodes and he drenches me with his cum. "No one else makes me come so damn quickly," he adds with a laugh.

"You'd be a piss-poor Incubus if they did," I retort with a chuckle and push him off me. "See you later."

It's his cue to leave.

I ignore his brief forlorn look as he re-clothes himself. I have somewhere that I need to be, and I have a stop to make on the way.

I throw him a bone. "I'll come find you later. Now go."

He beams at me and bows, "Yes, Your Majesty."

I roll my eyes at him. Only he can make it sound like he is mocking me. "Why do I keep you around?" I ask, bending down to pick up a human thigh bone from the middle of the floor that Musmortus has slobbered all over. I throw it back to her, but she is too busy giving Drescal the evil-eye to notice.

"Because no other male down here can fuck you like I do," he says darkly and then he sweeps out, his coat majestically swishing behind him.

I growl at him. He got the last word and that pisses me off. If I wasn't already running late, I would go out there, drag him back and let him see the business end of Babe.

I slam the door shut and head for the en-suite. I have to shower, get dressed and see Shax before my appointment.

* * *

I don't bother knocking as I barge into my twin's room that is situated a few doors down from mine. It used to be next door, but he got tired of listening to my screams of pleasure. His words, not mine.

I stop short of slamming the door shut behind me as I take

him in. He is naked to the waist and has his wings out. Black feathers flapping lazily, causing his hair to stir gently. He gets those from his dad, Dashel. The second ever Angel to fall from grace. The first, of course, was my great-grandfather, the original Lucifer. *My* wings are made from fire and they can burn a Demon from several feet away.

Shax turns towards me with narrowed eyes. He knows it's me and he doesn't bother to fold his wings back in, nor cover up the fact that he was about to screw some female. His wrist is slashed, his dark red blood dripping onto the carpet now.

I give the female a look of utter disgust.

Shax's blood burns Demons. But he uses it during sex as some kind of game. They line up for it, reveling in the scorch marks that it leaves on their skin momentarily.

I don't have a problem with pain, especially during sex, but I do have scorn for any bitch who comes sniffing around my brother. He is aloof, mysterious, eye-wateringly powerful and, not said in a creepy way, he is fucking gorgeous. The females eat it up around here.

"Belle," he says in that quiet, level tone that is his trademark. He never shouts, never whispers. "What's up?"

I gesture to the door for the bitch to leave, which she does hastily. Shax gives me an annoyed look, but then puts his wings away and does up his pants.

"So sorry for interrupting," I say, sarcasm dripping from every word, "but I need you to help me keep looking."

"Now?" he asks.

"In a bit. I have an appointment, but I wanted to make sure you carved out the time later."

"Fine," he huffs.

"Shax," I bark at him. "It's important. You know how much I need to find it. Find *him*." I look down, the feeling of guilt overwhelming me. I shove it aside as I have no place for guilt. Not even for this, but it keeps popping up like an irritating Hell-pit fly.

"I do, but our mother was very explicit. She said you had to wait a year and it's only been six months."

"I don't care," I hiss at him. "He did this for me, and it worked. Now, it's time to bring him back."

He gives me that mild look that crosses his face whenever my temper zings up a notch or two. I don't scare him. I can't hurt him. Even if I could, I wouldn't. I take a deep breath and count to three, then give him a bright smile.

He rolls his eyes at me. "Therapy in practice?" he asks with a smirk.

"Yes," I say steadily. "And I'm late for it, so promise me, you'll meet me in the dungeon later."

"Much later," he replies with a yawn and flops back to the bed.

He is asleep within seconds.

"Great," I mutter and head out to my appointment, over half an hour late.

About the Author

Eve is a British novelist with a specialty for paranormal romance, with strong female leads, causing her to develop a Reverse Harem Fantasy series, several years ago: The Forever Series.

She lives in the UK, with her husband and five kids, so finding the time to write is short, but definitely sweet. She currently has several on-going series, with a number of spin-offs in the making. Eve hopes to release some new and exciting projects in the next couple of years, so stay tuned!

Start Eve's Reverse Harem Fantasy Series, with the first two books in the Forever Series as a double edition!

Also by Eve Newton

https://evenewton.com/links

Printed in Great Britain
by Amazon